Exodus.

<u>OTHER KOKOPELLIMA PRESS BOOKS BY ANGEL BRYNNER</u>

Eutaxis　　　Ecclesia　　Exodus

Erebus　　　　Exist　　　　Esthesis　　　Epicharis

Elision　　　　Elysum　　　Empyrean

<u>AOLAB active art decks & books BY ANGEL BRYNNER</u>

ZION　　　HALCYON　　　DELUGE　　　BLOOD OF MY BLOOD

FLESH OF MY FLESH　　BONE OF MY BONE

BLACKWATER　　　OVERFLOW　　　EDEN　　　ZENITH

<u>AOLAB Travelogues BY ANGEL BRYNNER</u>

BOTTOM OF THE NINTH WARD BULLETINS

BLACKWATER RISING

<u>Anthologies BY ANGEL BRYNNER</u>

FIRESTARTER　　　FIREWALKER

<u>Grievechronic Revisionist AOLAB Active-Art books by Angel Brynner</u>

DELUGE, ZION, HALCYON BLOOD FLESH& BONE ZENITH

Exodus.

/grievechronic\

Angel Brynner

KOKOPELLIMA PRESS
MOAB · NEW ORLEANS
KOKOPELLIMAPRESS.COM

Library of Congress
Cataloging- in- Publication Data Brynner, Angel
Exodus, grievechronic/ Angel Brynner

Audiobook edition
ISBN: 978-1-950077-34-2
Copyright © 2024 Angel Brynner

Third edition
ISBN: 978-1-950077-63-2
Copyright © 2024 Angel Brynner

First edition
ISBN 9780991153114
Copyright © Angel Brynner 2003
Library of Congress Control Number: 2014958919

Cover and book design by AOLAB. Additional artwork credit:
Macrovector/Freepik, rawpixel.com/Freepik | Freepik AI

KokoPelliMa Press
MIAMI   NEW ORLEANS
KOKOPELLIMAPRESS.COM

Exodus.

To set the captives free.. you Have to start to really see.

The ultimate beginning ..
.demands an end as its origin.

For Love.

chapter one

Every blink of her eyes on her way to the subway station, Artyo had been accosted with the love of her life preparing for suicide 8000 miles away, too much of a coward even in his darkest hour to do it to himself in solitude. With every flicker of darkness descended, he shrieked across internal sectors as if her blinking were the equivalent of reed lashes against the flesh of his back. He screamed out that he had been able to hear her the whole time, admitted only as he aggressively searched out death. Knowing she would not be able to tear her eyes away, to ignore it as those around him pretended to. Because he knew she loved him. And now knew how much he loved her too.

She came out of her daze on the steps leading down to the subway. Her fingerprints invalid and stolen id chip denied, she searched through her pockets for the extra that she knew was not there as the train made its way into the station. The stench of the platform soaked into her as she stood pressed against the clammy tiles on the paying side of the gates, eyes splayed open as her last crossing with Thyaz re-reeled itself repeatedly, lurching in time to the sound of rickety trains on opposing tracks.

Together. Sprawled at a bar in Tokyo. Genetically manipulated sushen- the fake fish fleshed out with humano/bovine DNA that the surrounding sea had to be refilled with after the last major cult strike against the food supplies of Japan- zoomed past on plate after barely digestible plate.

There was a greenish glare due to individual digi-screens suspended in front of each climate-controlled stool.

English sub-titles flew past detailing a string of copycat high school sword attacks against the hateful teenagers that ruled over classmates. The fervor of the press ensured that the kids would continue to see slicing someone with their great-grandfather's sword as a viable way to regain family crest honor that had been wiped out with the war.

With lazy athletic movements Thyaz rudely grabbed plate after plate, spilling soy sauce on plaid pants she had sewn together by hand, blood from her own veins the only talisman protecting his ass on a day to day basis. His almost emaciated frame ruined the engineering of the cut in ways that were more insulting to her than anything stupid he said to her.

Across from them, less than lovely office girls droned on in matching tea serving uniforms padded out across the hips and cut to accent breasts too big for their frames. Their baby-like voices whirled as mechanically as the conveyer belt under the food zipping past in front of them, in heated discussion about the virtuous undertones of the most recent burning bed incident in the outskirts of Atsuji, Japan, another "un-fit wife" grown so tired of waking up to beatings that the wife had soaked his urine-stained futon with gasoline, let it air dry and then set him aflame in his sleep at the closing of the hour of the tiger, with all the possessions he'd bruised her over. The office girls preened themselves in hopes of catching the eye of whichever of the gaijin pair openly paid them any mind first. The details of the bizarre pictures the office girls painted became the background to Thyaz's theatrics, swung out in time to the clicking of the packed train she couldn't muster the energy to hop the turnstile and dash into.

She blinked and saw the features of the dull-eyed Japanese woman as they had cast her, late thirties, on her knees again

at 3am, trying to wash the smell of dried piss and regurgitated alcohol off of his best summer wool suit, trying to ignore the pain in her back from carrying him home again, trying not to touch the throbbing patch of skin across her cheek that she knew would keep her indoors and ashamed for most of yet another day. She used to be so beautiful, but ten years of cleaning him up after nights of puking alongside his office buddies had drained her soul just as much as being crammed sardine-like into the final train from Nishi-Shinjuku station in a show of terror-ridden camaraderie on the ladder of salariman success had drained his heart. The years of retrieving him in the dead of night after he'd stumbled into the right yards on the wrong streets played out inside of the poor, bent woman in Artyo's head, almost blinding her to the vulgarity of Thyaz, who sat impatient at her attention being elsewhere as his raunchy soy-stained drama gained speed.

He was cocky, knowing he wouldn't pay for a damn thing, without the sex normally tied to that arrangement for him in Tokyo. Starving after his money had been gone for months. The otokosans who had initially loved the curve of his instrument grew tired of his Oscar-vying oral performances in the bedroom. All his supposed "friends" vanished from his side when she had finally tracked down his crazily beautiful, broken ass.

Thyaz's mouth was full of food as he bitched about how she knew he only really liked one kind of fish, jabbing her in her ribs with his elbow. Hair he never had let her touch was neatly slicked from his widow's peak to his crown, the remainder of his naturally curly locks yanked back into a Dominican ponytail that was fuzzy and full of lint as it snaked down his back like the gigantic phallus he went out of his way to be, not having been unbraided and redone in weeks from the look of it.

"-You're the only one who looks at anything besides my fucking face and shoulders anyway," he had laughed loudly. "And you never do your own hair your damn self-" he'd snarled in hindsight to the eyes that took all of him in as quietly as they always had. He had seen insult in silent observation as usual, and then was embarrassed at attempting to attack her for no reason.

"Like they give a fuck about my fucking hair- they want me to fuck them as soon as they - Fuck them-" Thyaz had sat trying to talk big on topics Artyo had long since grown tired of hearing his half-baked sentiments on.

Vat-grown rice stuck next to his mouth as he boasted at but not for her, without a dime to his name, rubbing her face in the trash he'd let himself become trying to prove himself to be as much "Just like everyone else-" as he possibly could, because he truly believed that had been the storyline Fate had sent him to Earth to pursue. And there was nothing Artyo could do about dragging his ass back until he had played it out to the fullest. Artyo had waited-or tried to wait for all of it to be over. As patiently as an entity like her could suffer shit like that. But that day, something had made her realize that, left up to him they'd be trapped on Earth forever. And the unconscious part of his ass was perfectly fine with it.

"The best way to fuck a man out of his manhood and money is to call his masculinity into question against your own..." Thyaz had choked confidently, eyes twinkling with the tears of a blocked air passage as his mind had wrapped around an old favorite topic. "Something your asexual ass somehow seems to do to me all the time-" He snorted.

She remembered how the sinewy silence that had been hers in the midst of that onslaught transformed itself. How the moment stepped into itself, and how her Ka stood up before she did.

In one second, the battered connection to her bizarrely beloved broke like a china cup that had been thrown against the wall too many times and survived, a cup that one day just gave way from being placed gingerly on a well-dressed table as guests streamed in for afternoon tea. She recalled the tone of his curses as she threw a cup of hot tea in his face and walked out, knowing it was the biggest murder his ego had experienced due to her.

Snapping out of it, Artyo was drawn back to the present by the sound of folks shuffling towards the turnstiles in a rush let her know a train was coming. Her eyes cased the crowd.

chapter two

Mr. Wall Street was headed back home to pick up something necessary for him to start his day. He ran down the stairs to wait in the throng that appeared out of nowhere and let him know a train was approaching. He began to sense something feeding off the fear he was trying to hide, feeling death's perversely feminine breath softly on his neck. Blindly, he pushed thru the turnstile. Artyo slid her hips snugly against his and sauntered into the subway car behind him.

The bad day he'd been having snapped into perspective as the doors closed and he spun around to face the personification of what had been riding him during the early overtime at his desk at work. He found himself almost eye to eye with her and felt his chest heave as he took in how impossible this innocent-eyed woman looked, openly staring back at him with a soft smirk playing across her face. He felt naked as her eyes took in the lines of his gray wool bespoke suit as if she had made it and he was wearing it wrong.

He believed himself belittled as she whispered "nice tie" more to herself than to start up a conversation with him, her eyes playing across the unintelligible glyphs that covered the silk as if she could translate what it said about him: that he put more time into his edgy unaffected look than anything else. In that moment, a voice inside of him pointed out that he had in effect paid for this little trip of hers, and the browbeaten expression coating his J Crew catalogue face bloomed into full-blown scorn.

She smiled in recognition of his latent realization and made her way into the next car, her nose passing within a centimeter of his, smelling him as if he were her last meal, daring him to say a word, like she knew there was no power behind that sneer that he hadn't already sold. The door jammed open as she made her way to the next train car. His eyes followed her as she got comfortable in the low seats before the casings readjusted themselves and slid shut, cutting her off from view.

Full-color ads hung from the ceiling of the train, selling ESL courses and beer, with Right-to-Life banners imploring MEN to stand up for their rights to take away their wife's right to not bring more kids into the world. Hostility hung in pockets of recycled air. Everyone on the train had a different paper pandering takes on the story in Cleveland to their respective portion of the masses.

Every time Artyo closed her eyes on the ride uptown, she was a child watching an adult Thyaz on a tiny TV, in a white room with no windows or doors. Thyaz was bingeing, club after club, bloodstained from the fights he kept picking. The only sound was an erratic heartbeat.

A homeless man came into the train car from the other end. His feet were covered with sores. Even in the stuffy heat he was swaddled in three layers of filthy winter coats with his pants tied around his head in order to beat the heat. He smelled like dirt, which was better than stale urine in molding wool any day. Everyone ignored him. He was so far gone that he even forgot to rattle his cup in anyone's face. He trudged past Artyo belligerently arguing under his breath with the guardian that was trudging beside him as invisible to everyone else as the homeless man was.

"I've told you for 55 years-" the old man groaned softly to the glowing being beside him who pleaded for him to put his pants back on. "I am not going to hell for not putting my pants back on-I isn't hurting nobody no more- Hell is you

being on my back all these years- about keeping my pants on -I don't trust you- you ain't from no kind of heaven I'm going to," the homeless old man sputtered softly. "I'm going to Hell? Hell is you on my ass-"

Over in the corner, a tiny Peruvian man turned up his battery-operated radio tuned to 1010-ten ten wins, NYC's premiere talk radio station. A shrill voice broke in over the civilized din of the community forum being broadcast in regards to the whereabouts of Artyo Jaymes.

"There have been sightings in London, Cincinnati, Tokyo, Barcelona, and Brazil-ALL within the past 24 hours -This is not a joke, people! There NEEDS to be Justice! This is Vigilantism, and it is not the answer!!" The man leading the forum sung out.

"Violence is not a game!" a woman yelled, like she had heavy hands that had beat down so many kids for no reason that they had been unable to stop shaking since the story broke.

"These adults are dead-DEAD!! Swarmed on by their now mostly grown children like locusts from the Bible! It's DEMONIC-demonic!! How dare they? Are we going to continue to allow our deranged children to openly applaud such hostility against -against the very fabric of our society? Cheer for the murders of the very ones who created them in the first place?"

"Does anyone care what happened to make these kids resort to this?" a staccato-voiced man snapped, fed up by the bogarting by Mother Bible Belt.

"Who cares?!They're kids out of time- Bad Things Happen! Even happened to me- you get over it- it's part of life- they need to grow up!!"

"They need to grow up? They're Dead- they killed the ones who'd eaten them alive, then themselves!" Staccato interjected.

"I have a question- what did you do as soon as you got some authority over anyone else? After you escaped the things you went through growing up-did you know How to do better or-" another female member of the panel asked as politely as possible.

"Who cares what horrendous things those people enacted against those kids in the past? The past is over! You gotta treat it like it's over!" Mother Bible Belt whipped around towards Politely. "And what are you trying to accuse me of?!" she screamed.

"No one's accused you of anything- but you sound like you're scared you may end up marked too-" a panelist snorted.

"Now wait a minute- that's enough!" The moderator tried to regain control of the table.
"Look! Kids can't be socially educated to resort to violence against their own parents- we can't let this happen!!!"

"We've taught them to resort to violence with everything else- we've let what moved them to it happen all the time. We've turned our eyes away from kids being attacked forever. This was bound to-"

"She's the oldest- she's the ringleader! If she isn't brought to JUSTICE –"

"She may already be dead somewhere- look how the cousins ended their lives-" Politely whispered.

"Oh, She's alive! And she must pay for these heinous crimes or it'll be the end of the World as we know it!" Mother Bible Belt hissed.

"Maybe it is time for just that to happen. For this messed up world to just...end." Staccato sighed.

"The Bible says whoever curses his mother or father must be

put to death! Honor thy mother and father! Do NOT murder!" Mother Bible Belt barked at Staccato.

"I-I understand you're upset m-Madam, but-" stuttered a charming old man who had been silent for most of the Forum, "In Mark 9:42, The God in that b-Bible you quote also says-' *But whoever causes the downfall ...of one of these little ones....'* and these were kids when this began- little kids, that is what everyone is tiptoeing around in this- '*little ones who **believe** in m-Me- it would be better for him if a heavy millstone were hung around his neck and he were thrown into the s-sea.*'

"Also says it in M-Matthew 18:6." Old man Mo continued calmly. Stunned, the entire forum went silent as the microphones picked up the rustling of pages being flipped.

"Is- a life addicted to drugs to cope- is that d-downfall? Hhow about no self-respect? S-seeking out a-abuse cause it's all-all you know- does THAT sound like it'd be a Down-ffall from what – a loving God would h-have on tap for a – world full of kids that h-he loved?" No one on the panel had an answer for him. "So m-maybe, just maybe these barely grown-up, broken, now dead kids had been down-falling for so long that they-"

The owner of the radio got bored and flipped to Hot 97.

chapter three

In the other car, Wall Street sat there with his guardians who'd been bored to death up to this point, begging him to follow her- to pick a fight- do something- anything to show that he hadn't sold out for a cubicle, no free time, and a crack habit. As he clutched at the empty vial that had gotten him through half his morning, middlemen gods he didn't even know he had spat at what he'd become, insulted with all the time and effort they'd put into such a pantywaist.

"At least a coward would have a passive -aggressive kneejerk reaction to what went down!" They screamed, a chorus from a Greek tragedy sung for his internal benefit. As Wall Street stood there trying not to listen, his mind's eye played over the features of her he hadn't even realized he'd noticed. The baleful look on her face didn't make it up into her child-like eyes. The fact that her being at eye level came from her short torso sitting atop the longest legs he'd ever seen. He was surprised at the detail with which he had etched the motifs of said jeans into his brain when suddenly two new thoughts exploded at the base of his skull.

"I know that face- "was pushed out of his mind by *"**Maybe she has some-** "*

It rocked his soul as the empty vial in his pocket seemed to splinter off under the pressure of his fingers. As he pushed his way through the now crowded car into the next, the train entered 14th street station. The fever for his drug brought a false fight into his eyes. The train heaved to a stop as everyone seated in Artyo's car looked up simultaneously, saw it was not their destination, and turned another page in their papers.

Artyo quietly made her way off the train. Before he could think to move, he found himself crushed within a throng of truant

Junior high-school kids pouring in as the doors opened and closed.

He saw her walking away on the platform. The sweats began as he dug his free hand into the overhead pole to steady himself, willing the hand to hold on, to make sure he got home to his stash. On that day, Wall Street owned that he was a junkie.

chapter four

Oblivious to the sounds around her as she headed up the halls that led to the street, Artyo's mind completed their final time together to the sound of feet moving en masse in different directions.

She saw Thyaz looking around sheepishly, not even bothering to get up.

The arrogant smirk of "She'll be back-" splayed across his features like a child who didn't know any other way to keep her attention besides making her seethe and slap him. How that faded as the sushen he really did not normally eat began to jump nervously in his stomach with each moment that passed without her return. His face growing ashen as it dawned on him that he'd never see her again.

The digi-screen next to him loudly hummed with the sound of a woman moaning rapidly above J-pop guitar antics as the commercial for that month's prime-time sexed-out serial **"Tokyo decayed-decadence revisited,"** stunned the establishment to silence.

The well-known Japanese actress crawled around on her hands and knees, intricate patterns knotted into the ropes encircling her naked body at the feet of a lightly graying, handsome Gaijin man. A browbeaten voyeuristic salariman watched from the window across the way, reminiscent of the movie Rear Window. The woman turning out to be the wife of the salariman's most distinguished boss.

Thyaz's disgust for the impressionable things he had come to know the Japanese to be soaked up the hurt and rage he harbored for his soul-mate, seeing all the love affairs that would jump off due to the masses being inoculated with this newest mind-numbing krill. Artyo had finally done as he'd been passive-aggressively bemoaning her to do forever. She'd left him there to die versus begging him to come back for the umpteenth time, heart-broken enough to believe he wanted to be as far from her as earthly possible. She saw his brain as it found the solution in the crosshatching together both aspects of his current situation. She saw him zeroing in on the salariman stranger on the other side of him, who was all business and atrophy in his badly fitting "Wednesday suit," laid out by the woman he turned his check over to each month.

She pictured Thyaz stunning the slack-jawed stranger who stared back into the suddenly unveiled beauty of an evil fallen angel like a deer trapped in headlights. A hapless new victim unaware of the dirty scrawl of hair behind the halo of light shining out of Thyaz's face, or the stains on his once perfectly tailored pants that his chicken legs now swam within the folds of.

Artyo's jaw tightened. She pictured the stooped salariman whose life got overwhelmed by the envy other Japanese men and women would show after seeing him socialize with this beautiful Gaijin specimen. Her pace quickened as the shaft of light and fresh air came into view. In her mind's eye, the worn-down salariman's head bobbed up and down furiously, agreeing to do whatever the foreigner asked as long as he walked around with him, before Thyaz even opened his mouth to officially charm him in Japanese that he went to great lengths to make sound broken.

As Artyo spaced out at the bottom of the stairs leading aboveground, she knew it was too late. Rays of smog- filtered sun made fractals on the tile-lined walls leading up to Union Square. People pushed past, walked through her.

She swooned like a drunk when the rage hit.

Everything he'd thrown at her to deny what she had seen in him sucker-punched her in the chest. Air passages closed in her.

She wheezed against reality. The stairs threw up dust in response to the force of her steps. The summer smog made the NYC skies a metallic white that dragged through intense mid-morning heat. She purposely exited across from the decayed hull of the coffee shop restaurant on 17th, forcing herself into the crush of things one more time to remind her what she would be escaping at sunset.

chapter five

Hezuz stared at the image that bounced off the polished glass approvingly. His floor to ceiling windows had the best vantage point awarded to any being that had gained entry to the Empyrean, he had been told.

The afterglow of having rejected the newest batch of potential Almost-elohs(A/e's) made him blush malevolently as he looked out over but not at the city spiraling down below him. He inhaled the heady stench of emotionally broken, beautiful wannabe Elohs who had willingly submitted themselves to the spiritual whoredom of wandering around in his wake after he had not chosen them as his consort. His untouchable harem spread out around him. Their ranks were the best cloaked protective custody a cloistered chosen one like him could have ever dreamed for, if he remembered how to.

They fidgeted in the collective company that being christened an A/e demanded. The melanin-drenched shades of exposed skin on parade read like a painted desert. Perfectly applied blush gleamed on cheeks in the hothouse of Empyrean itself, women on the cusp of being surrendered to a frigid night none of them dared to think about. The effect was amped up by the pre-requisite white of their costumes in the harshness of the infrared light of Empyrean existence.

If he had not been such a spiritual cancer, he would have been fucking gorgeous. He had the big, sloe-like eyes of an entity who even after rebirth into the Empyrean, related to the universe through an almost predatory addiction to the feminine spirit. One so strong that his hazel irises had been re-calibrated and were now rimmed in the black of an unspoken infection accepted as the norm.

He was so unaware of his sickness showing that it had quietly turned in on itself and now feasted on him as prey instead.

He was drunk with power, wanton mouth set lopsided into the chiseled, burnt tawny face of a Sumerian son of god. Shiny, black, ribbon-like ringlets of hair befitting who he was groomed to become were clasped at the nape of his neck with a ribbon washed acid-white in sacrificial blood, playfully fleeing spirals here and there to beguile whoever had the blessed curse to take him in visually. His smile even bewitched himself when Hezuz saw the effects of it in the eyes of the ones who blindly auditioned to be the Eloh at his side at the end of times he had been told he would straddle like a colossus.

Already victorious in his mind's eye, he imagined life after the campaigns to plant the seeds for the hell that had to be sown on Earth before the kingdom of heaven could take root in the souls of those forbidden entry for past beliefs and arrogances. Hezuz was a professional. He talked with his hands like a persuasive pitchman. He moved his body like a gigolo practicing celibacy to gain an upper hand in his love affairs. He coated his delivery with mannerisms that amounted to nothing away from the audience but enchanted all. His performance was potent. He had no concept of the entities around him outside of servitude, educated to believe that the entire realm would look up to him once he quietly became king of a court no one realized they were being prepped to be the subjects of.

Something wired into every A/e exchange with him made the potential feel caught red-handed in the midst of sexual activity in a realm where such activity was maligned. The rejected ones residual humanity responded to his coyness.

The gaggle of A/e's blended into the overt furnishings of his ready-room. Not even trophies, they were the equivalent of wonderfully wrought wallpaper. Each hoped for even the slightest steady glance from him to wear amongst themselves, just as surely as they dreaded the possibility of whatever they sensed their presence around him meant to the repressed realm they moved in.

The A/e's were poured into painstakingly adorned dainty tops that showcased the perfected attributes once fervently prayed for below, their highest concepts of what heaven must have consisted of in light of the hell living on earth in the absence of the contours had been. Everything from heaving de´colletage to arresting falls of hair were presented in perfected shades and an inordinate amount of textures. Crystals and dots of white paste were placed precisely to draw attention to piercing eyes and bee-stung pouts. In intricately draped bustles, sarongs, petticoats and aprons hinted at the forgotten earthly portals to paradise that their ascensions into the Empyrean had made useless.

Hezuz had grown both weary and cocky in the attention of two-thirds of the Tryage and the A/e's they presented to him to pass the time, pantomiming perversities all the best puppet rulers on Earth actually got to participate in. In all the talk of impending heroics, spiritual wealth, and subjectivity First and Second Head filled him with, he became drunk with future-shocked power, understanding that they actually needed him to desire those things. He watched them bend over backwards at the hint of any boredom or indifference. He'd been used in many lives before this heavenly one, and an existence where someone was not trying to profit off of him was unimaginable. He was not as ignorant as First and Second thought. He was just so internally focused on something else that it read as the kind of stupidity the two Councilors needed.

Hezuz was only intrigued by the Third Head Councilor, the one who seemed unimpressed with him. The indifference in Third's occasionally unavoidable interaction with the to-be puppet king cut him even deeper due to the femininity of Third's aspect.

Numbness obviously cloaked as stupidity was why he finally received the vote from Third after the eons of back chamber politicking by First and Second to get preparations underway for the impending campaign. Numbness was something Third head could work with. Stupidity was not. A soul could be delivered from numbness by something as simple as a chase if it came down to it. But deliverance from stupidity was a conscious spiritual choice each entity had to make on its own.

First and Second Head were too indifferent to delve into the evolutionary difference between the two states, and they were too high off the perfected imagery Hezuz radiated, internally drunk off their own ideas of omnipotence over the situation. They behaved as if they had lined his features up Themselves.

"-Have the A/e's been calibrated for our little field trip?" First murmured. Second nodded yes as he gazed appreciatively on the perfection of the corralled entities around him. First Head clapped his hands together like an excited child.

Hezuz looked up from the thoughts of Third cloaked under layers of inner white noise. He beamed a loaded smile that had a Pavlonian effect on his surroundings as he made his way towards the doorway.

The flesh under his stenciled on stubble tensed as the A/e's whispered amongst themselves and followed in his wake, each A/e internally attempting to lay claim to the red on white pinstriped wool pants and shroud-like shirt picked out for the casual pomp and circumstance of the processional they all were to being led to. Being selected as an escorting A/e to an appointment such as this was taken as proof they actually had some effect on him.

The program was so simple that it was impossible for them to comprehend. They each took credit for his style due to the intimate suggestions they were collectively seeded with by the Tryage while in stasis. And they had foregone cross referencing with one another in the least in the quest to be crowned as his ultimate end-times consort.

Hezuz scooped up his whitewashed sacrificial palm frond slippers at the door and continued towards the outer concourse in his bare, prophetically glyphed feet to the sound of a collective gasp caught in the throats of the untouchable harem that shuffled into place behind him. As the A/e's with the large wooden basins began to toss rose petals in his path, The closest A/e to him offered her back as a means of support for him to slide into shoes she reasoned he must have forgotten it was necessary to wear when out in the realm out of a sudden outcropping of an old, ingrained habit of 'helps'. Hezuz looked through her as if she were contaminated by her own offer of assistance.

Bewildered, and hurt by the harshness of his refusal, she spun around, a shock of unsolicited hot tears threatening to explode from eyes that had supposedly had all tear ducts completely blocked. The faces of her fellow A/e's went dark with dryad-like envy before her, on the verge of tearing her to pieces out of rage, as if her actions hinted at a cloaked connect to him that none of them had been given. A pocket of space was made around her that quarantined her from their perverted fury and displayed her for all to see at the same time.

Punishers from the Pera sector slammed out of spirit into the atmosphere around them all and circled her like she was a rabid dog that had to be swept away before the line she had crossed even registered to the azure-eyed beauty. They punished the outbreak of burning bush like only they could. A nervous laugh escaped from deep within the A/e throng as the shock of how instantly that favela brush-fire had been put out. The smell of myrrh, aspic and asbestos flooded the nostrils of the A/e's as the Punishers evaporated as instantaneously as they had appeared. The white ash left on rose petals in the wake of firefighting overwhelmed some of the newly chosen as not-chosen accompaniments.

Somewhere deep within chambers, Third Head chuckled. Hezuz turned and dazzled First Head with a smile so bright that the Councilor had to slam his eyes shut.

Hezuz closed his lids in reply, to disguise the inward roll of his eyes under a heavy fringe of lashes. He dramatically dropped his heavy shoes to the floor with a loud thud and stepped into them through a cloud of evaporating rose petals and dust as if they were filled with shards of glass. He then turned and walked out into the red-soaked sky that bathed his outer terrace. First and Second head pulled their hoods into place and silently strode up beside him in time with one another. They motioned to the concubines to wait until they were called forth into the bright light.

"You understand the import of this incoming crop, do you not?" First Head intimated as his left hand absently searched in his hood for his refractors.

The whitewashed wool of his cloak was harsh to onlookers in the red light, on purpose. Hezuz smiled and gave all of his attention to Second instead of First, causing Second to pause as he pressed his own pince-nez refractors against the cartilage of his nose. He blushed under the weight of Hezuz's seemingly interested stare as First momentarily bristled at the smile being offered to his comrade and not him then cleared his throat, in protest.

"No- I do not understand the importance of any of these processionals, but that never has mattered before-" Hezuz Sighed.

"This time it matters, my boy-" Second beamed like a child.

"Yes- this time- this is the beginning of all we have prepared you for-" First whispered conspiratorially.

Hezuz's eyes lit up in surprise. "You mean it has begun? I-" the clarification of the confirmation got lodged in his throat. He laughed, his body actually felt warm for the first time, dead or reborn. His chest puffed up and his chin jutted out as if the promised crown had already been placed on his head.

"Let us walk-" Hezuz growled appreciatively into the glare of beauty he was indifferent to that surrounded him. He bounded down the stairs like a star quarterback charging out onto a home field. The glistening bodies of the A/e's snapped to attention as the sly nod of Second informed them that it was indeed time to begin their pilgrimage.

Like rivulets of chalky white water cutting into sandstone steps, the bevy of incomparable beauties belled out behind Hezuz and flowed down the stairs of his palatial compound in his wake. They cut into bustling streets that instinctively made room for them.

Droplets left by the bizarre downpour of mercury refracted the imagery of their procession back to anyone whose perfected vision dared to notice anything outside the direction of the highly favored Hezuz in the company of his chosen ones and two-thirds of the Tryage Council.

Bent over back after bowed head paused until the officials moved past, somehow knowing the Tryage to be incapable of physically looking back. They made their way through the crowds to the relic-like greenery of the Empyrean Gardens for the presentation of the Strands.

With each step, Hezuz gently pressed his tongue against the vein that snaked along the roof of his mouth that ended right between his two front teeth, letting hidden memories drip down and crash into his tongue, begging to be swallowed whole.

As the mind of Hezuz wandered through space and time back to where and what he was when all this began, nothing more than a splinter of the spirit of an abandoned boy carried up a ladder in the sky, his heavily hidden heart broke out into the craziest song.

chapter six

Union Square was packed. The network of streets from 23rd down to Ninth Street had become too weak to handle the buildings and the roar of MAC trucks long ago, and had been shut off to all but pedestrian traffic.

A labyrinth of unchecked commerce built up by demons of consumption had spawned itself throughout the district. The closest thing to a black-market this side of Hong Kong meandered across aisles the blocked-off area had been reduced to. Electrical cords snaked between plastic tarps overhead as the clapboard stands and makeshift tents wound their way through the ruins of the beautiful architecture that had once made this part of the city such a sight to see. People around her with too much money to spend and not enough love for the folks they were getting things for harassed bent folks who'd dealt themselves the hand of lowly booth man in the new bowels of NYC, profiting from satisfying the newest addictions that rocked the landscape around them as clearly as they lived trapped under the paw of it.

Artyo took it in for the last time. The sea of people parted around her as it always did, naming her as untouchable without clarifying if it was due to sanctity or strife. Light seemed to slice through the stalls spread out around her. Goods that were not supposed to be sold were hidden under the solar flare sensitive crap no one cared that they had.

The aggressiveness of Artyo's pace was checked and balanced by the passivity of hustlers in regards to her presence. No one who recognized her approached her. They were respectful of her once the fear at the base of their spines regarding what she was doing there passed.

It was what had honed in her a preference for them and their company, and the jarring feral beauty she saw in the realities of their various worlds.

She watched for the light to play off someone's face in the right way, the holy grail of sure things when on the lookout for whatever you truly needed, that every hustler spent his life searching for. She'd lived her life off those kind of lights at her best and worst, rode them like waves, and she was going to ride them to her final destination, thru final Puryf and then right off this Popsicle stand of a spiritual plain.

Artyo felt her pulse quicken the closer she got to pay dirt. She tried to entertain herself by dancing over the features of the only one she would say goodbye to, the sacred mute housed inside APC: Anya's Puryf Complex.

Another refugee- Azerbaijani via Israel. Beautiful. In the ways Thyaz was before he started to fuck up, before all the war paint had started to seep in. Her eyes slammed shut on the ocular comparison. As they reopened, her eyes fell upon the glistening baldhead of an Indian man with a hieroglyph of wings across his forehead in ochre two shades lighter than the rest of the skin. He sold books. In the midst of all this trafficking of contraband, women, children, medical procedures, organs and identities, the old Jain had the audacity to sell books.

They spilled out of his stand in every direction, bound in leather, fabric, or paper. Some were held together by rubber bands, some by shoelaces or bungee cord. Others were encased in layer upon layer of tape that would turn to dust under the slightest pressure. He was old and out of place at first glance, until you saw how the actual energy of the place erupted from his eyes, which she was sure no one trolling here ever did because only the rowdiest or most innocent Hustlers looked someone dead in the eye and dealt with what they saw.

He was her man.

When Artyo locked eyes with him, the only thing of import she saw was that he knew what she was.

" What do you have that I need-" she purred softly as she leaned over the pile of somewhat familiar titles as if she'd take whatever it was if he dared not to give it to her. The knots on her temples from the Anjuge throbbed as if they had just been re-smacked. The old Jain leaned away from her prying eyes as if the face of Shiva had just shaken him from a dream he had really been enjoying.

"Depends ...on what you have acquired as of late that is worth my time and energy" He whispered coyly as he shifted on his sits bones. The only other muscles that moved were in his eyes, cutting to the left of him. With a flick of her wrist, she tossed the tiny coin she had stolen from the old crone. He scanned her as if seeing the self-actualized entity she no longer had any clue that she was.

Without a word, he activated what would take her home by dragging the coin in a petri dish of blood that sparkled like crushed rubies. The one coin separated into three that absorbed all the sacrificial blood. He smiled, activated the Directory Assistance Peripherals that would give her entry into the realm of the being the shimmering blood belonged to, dragged two of them in wax and passed them back to her with the third coin.

"What were you called?" she queried, finger tracing Stars of David absently into the cover of a worn copy of The Fountainhead by Ayn Rand that had been given choice positioning on the table.

"Was? Still Am. Magii." The old man replied absently. "My

fee?" he said, mind slicing through any more questions to what was of most import to him at the moment.

Artyo grabbed him by the ears and shoved the third coin against his teeth with her tongue before letting him go, a gentle smile on her face. He ran his tongue over the surface of the ancient currency as if his mouth was outfitted with the newest of scanners already here in the stalls a year before they'd go mainstream. His vision blurred as memories of his own connect to where the coin had come from sung out of his spirit.

She pocketed the D/A.

"Have fun storming the castle-" The Magus whispered, drunk off inner mnemonics as Artyo disappeared into the crowd.

chapter seven

Hezuz's cloaked thoughts trembled inside of him.

A secret made his heart blush under impending things. He sung out lopsided serenades inside. Aimed at the one he'd been so privately addicted to below from above that he had reached out to her through the latent realities of anything that had even absently caught her eye, before she began to catch onto the familiarity of his spiritual scent within each set of limbs she had found herself temporarily entangled with. Including momentarily through the one called Thyaz, before Thyaz's Ka reared up in protest, without either party being the wiser regarding the possession that their affair had begun through.

She was his One below, his secret, found from sifting through the ashes swallowed by him as he came of age as a royal Empyrean child, the sickness haloing his Hazel eyes for any with wherewithal to see. The joyful sounds in his insane inner world echoed like crunching chips against sensitive teeth. His One. His crazed One. The One he had never known outside of his heart and head, but knew better than he had ever known himself, even in the afterlife. Burning towards him like a comet, right as First and Second aimed at the throne.

I see you-in the weight of the early clouds of morning, the hand of god covering your eyes, hidden away-i am going to cleave with you in the worst way. walk barefoot thru your halls. burn fear into those who wronged you. by my existence, utterly in love, alone. i have waited, wading through this energy called you your entire life, unknown, the true threshold of me.

i am left naked in my own eyes, rocked with gratitude by the journey taken, equipped for receipt. softened by the expanse of poetry that has shot out of me due to the impending prosperity of me with you. they fall in love with the energy of me due to how blatantly it is meant for you. they covet what you have called to yourself, spotless, blameless, clean. Demand it, even in this forsaken space, words flowing around me, so pretty that i shy away from them, worried you may laugh, or understand, and make me cry. my faith is in a god this realm denies, but the inevitability of you to me proves. the works of my word spring forth , melancholy music no more, bluntness wrapped up in his sweet revelations. love held pristine as i could. heart hurts, chest shaking, pain overshadows childbirth, horizon. growing pains in the outer limits of my heart, behind the thick of Empyrean clouds, make your way, knowing you hear me, understanding the humanity in us all, and how it cracks and claws until the strength in us buckles. the rest of your final night is me whispering to you on levels even you do not know exist, all the way through. remnants of imagined days spent against the soft swell of your breasts, imagery that coats me and keeps me clean, indifferent to all else. i hurt from the lockdown of loving you from so deep that it awakens an intimacy with the love of heavenly hosts himself, showing me my love as is and as of, outside, situations and sacrifices, consuming all the small, hard things once allowed to matter. You. barreling towards. releasing the energy of the love and locus of me- I can look on stupidly at things, alive by the breath of you crossing for me, unbeknownst to even you. just for the taste of your tongue playing across my lips. even if the attempt itself will bring on an Armageddon like these devils cannot even conceive in all their perceptions of perfection and paradise.

I honor the beauty of life, and from a true God, unseen, i simply request the love and the companionship of you. they can have everything else. Just come for me. the prater-joys of you, faith burnished to its most resplendent, in love. your arms around me as you fall, pangs echoing inside my chest like creaking joints on long-closed doors, letting you in wholeheartedly all the same. i want to cry out in the here and now, let you rock from the pangs of ecstasy that wish to destroy me with their power, untamed, the god in me that rose up to the call of you in the earliest hour.

i wish you were sprawled across my bed, even if it had to be on fire, fully clothed, but naked in the honesty of things pouring out of you into the cup of me. pretty things against the roof of my soul, cloudbursts burning off the enmity, love as it was meant to be, no sin in accepting how after-life feels lived when i think of love, you.

With a flicker of his Empyrean-focused outer eyes, Hezuz clocked how close they were to arrival at the Gardens and smiled out to a First and Second as they gobbled up the shock and awe of the Empyrean Citizens their procession pushed through, pleased with the sounds of crunching corn chips that reverberated in the space Hezuz's signal filled in their heads.

chapter eight

Artyo carefully stuck the D/A/P to the small of her back with a few pieces of sheer micro pore tape from her bag. She looked up at the sky, gauging her estimated time of arrival at Anya's complex. She pushed onto Ninth Avenue, her reflection bouncing across the mirrors that lined the fences around construction sites.

The closer she got to Anya's, the more uncomfortably the D/A/P dug into her back and the more her temples throbbed. Waiting for the elevator to the 13th floor was the worst. As she raised her finger to the buzzer, she realized she'd forgotten to take any blockers.

"Fuccccccccccccck-" she whimpered into Anya's smiling face.

The woman smirked in acknowledgement that there were no painkillers anywhere near this one who could not handle in-house injections, which meant they were all about to go through hell. The clip to Anya's Trinidadian tongue rung out full-force.

"You do dis on purpose-" the woman began as she snapped her fingers. Anya's two male assistants appeared to help Artyo out of her gear. "You're dat word! - Syphen, what was dat word guest Zensan used earlier?"

Syphen looked into Artyo's eyes through a face with no eyebrows or lashes, the smile that didn't show on his lips in the presence of his boss slut-dancing in his eyes. "A MASOCHIST, Anyasan." He said curtly as he slid the satchel off of Artyo's shoulder.

"Yes! Masochist- that's what you are, a masochist!! You cry

like a baby every time, even hocked full of blockers and killers, and whatever else you -you avoid-dis- ME-and den NOW- you return t' us- right before you have t' depart, right? And you don't even have the decency t'med yourself up a bit . .. so all of Us- has t' hear you scream-"

"Why are you complaining, Anya? Isn't pain your 'Ting'? You're paid on retainer whether I roll through or not!" Artyo glowered. "Besides, this is the last time. I need every aspect of me awake-damn kill me if you have to- To the quick- til you yourself can see that the very last of me is up-ioncare, yall can deal with seeing a few tears-"

"Screams! They'll be SCREAMS-Art'yo-" Anya laughed loudly. "Like you in labor, cryin all over mah-"

" -Mmmaybe it's the only time I get to cry..." Artyo grumbled. " This time, I need you to be as sadistic as you obviously got into this racket to be-" Artyo chuckled harshly. Syphen stifled a laugh as his partner Marok openly snorted.

Anya eyed the embarrassed Marok disapprovingly before she turned and walked down the hall." -Jus for dat one, I won't show you Nan a mercy...cut'er out of dat shit-" the woman called over her shoulder. Artyo glared at the still blushing Marok as he and Syphen box-cut her pheromone-soaked clothes off of her in the foyer.

"I'm always amazed at what you have on under your clothes-" Syphen slurred seductively into her ear as he carefully cut the D/A/P off of its perch with a tiny scalpel affixed to his index finger. His mouth was suddenly thick with the obscure accent he was usually pained to keep hidden.

"What's zis?" he asked, the activated D/A/P balanced in the palm of his hand, eyes wild with curiosity.

Before she could answer, Marok cut the shoulder seams of her tank open with no warning, inadvertently rendering her topless except for the forearm he quickly encircled her with in order to avoid as much impropriety as possible. A dark look danced across his face at his own misgauge.

Artyo had put out of her mind what had brought her there initially.

A lifetime ago on her first weekend in the city, she'd found her legs wrapped around the head of a Kouros-looking boy in the infamous bathroom of Gatien's Tunnel. The color of raw honey, he brought to mind the mouthy decadence of baklava. His hair curled up on itself even tighter than hers and its presence made the reality of him as a worker for Anya all the more bizarre later on. They'd parted ways without so much as an exchange of syllables, let alone nicknames.

Days later, riled by the unfulfilled after-heat that was characteristic of her in those days, she had spotted him on the street ducking into the building this complex was hidden in. Like a panther that liked the smell of only a certain kind of prey, she had entered the empty lobby, watching the elevator stop on the 13th floor and return to her. She had strode into the elevator with the bawdiness of a cowboy and pressed the 13th button as the doors closed, totally blindsided by him as he had tackled her to the ground, paranoid, his eyes wild, silent.

Artyo had let out a squeal of laughter that he had slammed his hand over her mouth to silence. His nose recognized the aroused smell of her before his eyes re-adjusted to the sight of her from the weekend before. He had grinned, nostrils flaring, but had not said a word.

Still muffled and aware that he was indeed reacting to the scent of her as much as she was to him, Artyo had asked him his name. He pointed to a small tattoo on his right forearm that said Marok. He then held her down on the floor of the tiny elevator with one arm as he reached over to the control panel, pressed cancel and then the emergency stop button. She recalled the curious look in his eyes as he tried to figure out what her reaction would be after the fact. Artyo had known he was tall enough to make her have to tilt her head up slightly to lick at his ear. She dealt with him being ample enough to pin her down with no issue as well. The curve up from the small of his back to his shoulders had felt like marble warmed by blistering heat. He had the foul, fleshy mouth of a sailor. He had kissed her softly as he tucked her hair behind her ears, the heaviness of him pressing her into the corner of the suspended elevator so roughly that her first ever black-girl bruise would form later and not fade for weeks. Even now Artyo could not recall what she had worn, only that somehow it was off and he was in her in ways the twisted virginity of her lost sense of as she was straddling him with her hands wound in his wild hair.

Marok had skipped work that day, took her home with him in silence. They were together for two months without ever speaking a word to one another. All communication between the two had been physical or visual. A touch, letters, notes, a caress, snarl, a tackle. There was laughter-lots of silent laughter.

It was like he was possessed by something greater than the both of them, older- ancient almost. His hands in, on and around her had honed things inside of her that still made her shiver.

It had ended when she wanted to leave and whatever was riding him thought he could make her stay by saying her name, through him, against the will of his blocked vocal chords, calling after her.

He wouldn't be able to forget the confused look on her face due to the sound of his voice for many years, but not as many as it took for her to escape the sound that echoed out of him where his voice should have been. She looked as if she had heard God speak her name. But what had thrown him had been the nature of what hearing that had brought out in her face, as if she'd heard her own voice on an answering machine for the first time ever. And it was the first time he realized that she was a baby that she didn't yet know what she truly was.

Years later on her last day in the cage, the recall of it all flashed between the two of them in an instant.

Artyo ordered Syphen to store D/A/P in the vault, to toss her satchel and gear she'd worn into the incinerator, and to retrieve the last set of gear she had stored there. As he turned to go, Artyo's lips landed softly on the forehead of her first lover.

"I'm not coming back this time," she murmured into his ear. "You never belonged here as it is-" he mouthed silently against the hollow of her throat. Sensing where her thoughts were headed by the throb of the emotions trapped behind the thin gash across her throat, Marok cut her a dirty look, baring his teeth as if he'd rip her arm off if she even so much as touched him where she was thinking of at his place of business, in front of his boss.

Artyo grinned slyly, stepping into the center of the room and up into the brace.

As she slipped fingers and toes into the appropriate grips Syphen swooshed in and tightened the cuffs at her ankles and wrists as Marok backed away.

"-Well," Anya murmured approvingly as she floated into the room and circled around Artyo like a vulture about to swoop down on a fresh kill. "It seems that you have done a little handiwork of your own very..." Anya purred, caressing Artyo's still tender neck, "...recently." she finished, flicking it. Artyo winced in pain.

Syphen and Marok stood to the left and right of Anya and awaited her command. "Are you ready?" Anya asked plainly as she placed the protective blinders over Artyo's eyes.

"Of course not-But go! Do it anyway-" Artyo whimpered as Anya gave the nod.

"Fade out." Anya commanded. Syphen and Marok coated Artyo with a mixture of rock salt, avocado oil, sugar, and charcoal, scrubbing her as if they were pulling the devil out of her pores.

She started to black out due to the scouring sound the metal sanding surfaces of the gloves they wore made as they ripped across topical scars and piles of dead skin leaving tiny streaks of blood across her backside and thighs. Artyo roughly screamed and passed out.

chapter nine

A small child was once again curled up in a bruised ball, tangled in white hair. One of the ones who refused to be refused. Something behind her almond-shaped eyes slid back and forth under her lids, rhythmically following the shadows of those hurting her with no cause, mapping out their fighting styles for future reference, gritting her teeth at how they always hit the same place, spaces along her emaciated body that had gotten tough, bones broken so many times that they may as well be steel, unbeknownst to her attackers.

The child blinked, catching sight of Artyo in what looked like shackles off to the side. Artyo screamed again and all abuse against the child stopped. White hair pulled away from her body like a cocoon unraveling as the little girl's eyes popped open in a white empty room. She blinked again, looked in the opposite direction and, bewildered, saw Artyo being flagellated, skin cells systematically shorn from her with precise motions.

Instead of fear, a strange calm came over her as she understood that Artyo was not shackled like a prisoner at all, that the abuse was consciously chosen, and that this was the child's prayed for window of opportunity.

Something inside of the chest of the little girl exploded where her heart used to be. She rubbed her eyes like it was Christmas, walked over, curled up at Artyo's shackled feet like she was home and passed out.

chapter ten

"Record time," Syphen called out.

Artyo woke up and partially blacked back out to the sound of Anya's laughter. The blinders had been removed for stage two when she came back to.

Laughing hysterically, she took in the oversized equalizing acupuncture quills sticking out all over her, one per square inch, even on the soles of her feet. She looked like a future-shocked porcupine strung up on a spit for roasting. Artyo was damn near delirious due to having never gotten this far without breaking in the past. The quasi-lockdown of the space during session ensured that none of them had a clue what had made her strong enough now, and the concern covered every inch of Marok as he watched her de-fragment fully for the first time.

"Pay her no mind," Anya said absently in reply to the surge of worry that made its way to Marok's face due to Artyo's unhinged guffaws of laughter.

"She's giddy from arriving all the way- Tis a variant of the shock. I told you she would eventually. Come now, she's fine." Anya clipped as Artyo lost all that was left of her mind.

chapter eleven

Silky white hair clumped like the bars of a cage. Another of the refused to be refused, tortured for her spiritual insolence.

Don't cry, take it, stronger than they can ever be-" Artyo gritted her teeth as she whispered to the child again and again.

The child started to blink slowly, seeing the body attached to the voice comforting her between her lashes, with what look like porcupine quills stuck up and down her body, suspended in the air- Laughing.

Bewildered, the child's eyes snapped all the way open in shock, and she peered at the woman in hysterical pain in front of her as a mixture of bad blood and oil rose up and dripped from the wounds the needles made in her flesh. A spirit of peace descended on the child and the tangled bars of hair yanked back as if doors to a jail had been roughly flung open to set the prisoner free.

The little blushing bruised black child with the halo of white hair wildly laughed along with Artyo as she crawled over and lay down at her feet next to the bruised little girl already by her and fell into a deep sleep of her own.

chapter twelve

"Fohn out. " Anya commanded.
The centralized air system whirled into action, drying the red-tinged sweat that flowed from every pore of Artyo's now purified body.

The three swarmed her. In seconds she was coated from her hairline to the tips of her toes in hot wax, screaming like a banshee as it was ripped off with strips of fabric in various directions at the same time. The surface of Artyo's skin went into shock from being too traumatized to know where to hurt first.

"Fall out." Anya ordered.

Torrents of rain whipped and whirled around a blinded Artyo, alternating from hot to cold, as the suddenly enclosed space began to fill, submerging Artyo completely in water as the light in the space was blacked out. The embryonic regeneration therapy held her under water until the pressure made whatever was left within her heart completely capsize and float up to the surface of her mind, will, and emotions.

chapter thirteen

Another child materialized.
Behind her was all white. In front of her, Artyo thrashed underwater. Unconscious, the little girl levitated the way Artyo seemed to in the chamber and flipped upside down. She was pulled to her place between the other two children who had finally found solace at Artyo's feet.

The eyes of the little girl popped open. She knew she was drowned, but was somehow still alive.

Washed up on a riverbank, out of waters teeming with what looks like white seaweed. She stood in front of a box rammed full of naked, crying kids. The kids started screaming at her as a bell chimed in the distance.

"Run!!Before it's too late!!"

She took off for the trees, looking behind her at the river, and ran smack dab into the calves of a man and a woman that hadn't been there when she had first taken off. Terrified, she started to cry.

"What are you doing?!" The kids in the box on the riverbank behind her screamed, unable to see the couple towering over the little girl.

"Shh~ Don't cry-don't worry-" The couple whispered to her as they both bent down to her level, each kissing away tears that streamed down either cheek. She got up, looked at them in confusion, then back at the river in time to see a cluster of women in black shrouds slither into the river from the other side, then rise up to walk across it, instantly dry as the children in the cardboard box howled.

The little girl took off for the cover of the trees again. The couple showed up beside her and slammed a hand over her mouth before she could think to scream.

"Those out on the river can't see us. You can. Because you're Ours-You're safe-We've been waiting so long for you-" they whispered again and again, and rocked her to sleep in their arms. All three disappeared in the shadows of the trees moments before the old Queen, the one covertly called the Anannke showed up.

The voice of every child got trapped in their throats as the old Queen glided through the cloud of women shrouded in black that pressed around the cardboard box hungrily.

The old lady rammed her hand into the clutch of cowering children and picked up a kid that looked remarkably like the little girl who had just washed ashore and ran. She held her up overhead, snapped her spine, and threw her roughly to the ground. The shrouded women cheered ecstatically.

"...Carry on." The old queen whispered and rose up, in cloaking shafts of light, to the horror of the shocked kids.

Construct mothers picked out their newest whipping children and disappeared, leaving twelve of the twenty-four children that had been rammed into the box like sardines behind.

chapter fourteen

Artyo woke up and passed out again.

When she came to the third time, heavy hot stones were strewn across her body, which was flattened out on the floor. The three girls curled up around her in her mind's eye watching her breathe steadily, until one by one, they kissed her on the head and faded from sight.

Upon completion, Marok carried her back to the preparation area. Syphen talked Anya out of the complex for a food binge, so the two were alone.

Marok anointed her with myrrh, spikenard and eucalyptus oil as she slept with her newly waxed thumb in her mouth. He kneaded the skin on her temples. She awoke curled up in his lap. He was the only person in NYC that she'd felt she had to say goodbye to and he knew it. Artyo crawled away from him, pausing to look at him one more time, bashfully wondering if her time this afternoon would be best spent under him.

"Don't even think about it," he whispered, the trumpets of an instantly patched-in Hezuz blaring where the once sacred mute's voice should have been. Hezuz fought to have his say between the thoughts of Marok, knowing what she was thinking.

"Because if you did, I wouldn't let you leave-" Marok mouthed. Artyo looked away as he watched her from the floor. "Although maybe, that is exactly what you need, huh? Someone who would not let you leave?" Hezuz sung softly to her through Marok as he moved towards her deliberately, easing his arms around her, pinning her to him tightly.

"Someone who'd make you stay just a little longer, grow a tad stronger ... hmmm?" He whispered into her hair. Artyo felt the muscles in her face tighten as she clenched her jaw.

"Just a little longer... Tenshi-" he murmured, running his fingers under her chin. The lights flickered overhead.

"-Is this what you came here for? To see him- I mean me, to see if you'd desire to come back to life?" She could feel the devilish grin on his face as he kneaded the words into her, daring her to blink, emotionally intimidating her the way he had taught her to intimidate others who'd wanted to steal pieces of her through the men he had fallen in love with her through.

"...Do you think-" he whispered, warm black eyes rolling shut as she pressed her back against him, "-That it would be- feel like it used to-?"

Suddenly Artyo stiffened, and craned her head to look at him curiously over her shoulder. "No-" she stated simply, the sound of dog-tags jingling inside of her head, "because this time I can't pretend it's not you talking through Marok to me like I can't tell the difference, like I don't know exactly who and what you are."

Marok sat there staring into her eyes, then pressed his lips against her right temple of his own accord.

"Well...will you stay with *me* for a while? I don't care what you did-" he whispered hoarsely, his throat catching on fire as he forced his own words out of his mouth, blocking out the "assistance" from above that had muted him a lifetime ago in the first place, long before she had ever crossed his path. The syllables he gave her brought blood the corner of his mouth as though he had swallowed jagged glass.

"How long." She whispered numbly, shocked at what they suddenly were in the midst of, feeling her weight in his arms."-How long?" she cried out, as if having to ask him again hurt her.

"I'll keep him away...if you'll have me...It won't be like swallowing silence this time-" he mouthed harshly, wrapping his arms around her even tighter as his curiosity at the texture of being inside her again awakened.

The shock at how large her eyes looked in the reflective surface of the anteroom passed as the dizziness of his entry into her died down. The shock at her realization that they were beautiful in motion did not. Artyo closed her eyes and listened for cherry blossoms bruising themselves against the pavement in the sleep his motion lulled her into.

Hezuz stood by and sung out like a thorn-bird as he watched Marok make love to the love of his after-life for the last time. His twisted spirit scrawled his song all over the two of them as they forcibly ignored him, blotted him out by the bombs of energy that went off up and down her spine with each caress, stroke and thrust made by Marok into her.

Artyo tried to block the beckoning of Hezuz, imploring her softly to let go and let herself feel who she had really been enthralled with all along, whispered against the hairline along the side of her forehead shamelessly.

i don't care - you sense me here. i want to lay my head next to yours and talk to you, drowsy off the smell of what is passing between us finally on the same plane, lucid due to what is coursing through. sectors of you. cajole me into consumption. try to deny me the closer you come-but you're mine, and the only one you have ever loved, through them is me. my heart and throat are coated with emeralds. my words sink into you, bells ring out inside of me, places open up that i never knew existed. my fingers placing thoughts behind your eyes. i thank god for the intent within me surfacing, punishing me for things i thought i controlled. Compromised, the sound of your groggy whisper will be indiscernible from my own. i won't flinch in awareness of you usurping my thoughts i won't laugh at you telling my jokes as if they were your own. the fight for sleeping closest to the edge will long since have died, you aggravate my sleepless nights... beside you, planting thoughts in your dreams as i play with the corners of your mouth. i love you for the rawness wrapped up in affections you've never had the chance to genuinely let out.

Marok reared up in protest as the press of the words into his flesh became unbearable combined with the sound of her breathing roughly against what may as well have been the both of them.

"Enough!" He rebuked the airwaves tangled around the two of them, his voice splintering against his teeth. Artyo grabbed his face.

"Focus!" she whispered. "I know the difference-I came here for it-" she growled softly. "I came here for you-now it's your turn to-"

As Artyo and Marok consciously came together the cloaked spirit of Hezuz retreated, nonplussed.

chapter fifteen

She couldn't stop smiling in the aftermath of experiencing the last drop of her humanity with the first entity that had affirmed the beauty of the inhuman woven through her. Artyo left a still-fighting-for-self-possession Marok naked and passed out.

She got dressed in what she'd decided to die in and made her way back out into the broken world for the final time.

Copper spirals she had wound around her own ring fingers in swirls of two and three gleamed pinkish as love stereo continued to scream Hezuz's chaotic cords, now in the tonalities of Thyaz from the jukebox of her heart. Hezuz amplified his heavenly vibration to ensure that the lover of Artyo he loathed the most would be violently cut down. Artyo attempted to block out what she took as the sounds of Thyaz's voice losing its mind with poetry of her own.

your face i don't see, streets empty, where our story should be, defiled the purest given, hatred, demon driven ,gates of hell, other side no soul resides, soul mate or not bond is dead picked the path you tread, i loved you no reason to take more, never appreciated it, ensure it's dead, Macbeth, hands bloodied, red, under my skin, won't let me be, will set, me free- under no longer whitewashed dreams, freedom pains you, hear your screams-

The straps of the quilted leather bulletproof vestyr she had lined with pinstriped blue pima cotton and slashed open to expose the upper flesh of her breasts fanned open in time to her step. The buttery black of the leather gleamed against her skin. The fishnet knibs that encased her arms stopped at the rim of cyclist gloves she had ripped the tips off of.

The chalk stripes she'd drawn by hand on the soot -colored thin flannel pants were positioned at third base, frayed at the waist and hem, looking as though they couldn't hang any lower on her hip or expose more of her fishnet trunks without being obscene. Curly chunks of hair spun out behind her in the wind as she made her way uptown. With each step that she took her entire body throbbed, words rumbling around in retaliation to the atmosphere around her and inside her head.

chapter sixteen

"There is something so wrong with my-I am so over this existence-"

The one called Gera scribed roughly into the padded walls of her soul/cell with charcoal that crumpled with under the force of each letter of the tag. Her blood-red obi embroidered with crows pinched her side as she slouched against the freshly drawn graffiti.

The sunset-hued kimono loosely secured under it shifted slightly open at her breasts, almost revealing them. She didn't notice. She was too busy. Indulging in the drunken despair she had been continually bathing herself in since the one she'd been appointed caretaker to had blatantly turned her back on the dominion and riches Gera had so graciously extended to her. Again.

"How dare she?" She moaned to no one in particular. "How could she stop at the gates of my paradise? How dare she turn and spit in my eye?" She roared.

Gera crumpled melodramatically towards the floor. Blackened wooly waves of hair spread out in every direction as her frame arched up through her elongated neck to the still- soft spot on the back of her crown. Her legs slid out in front of her, encased in the stockings of a circus trapeze artist and the discarded legs of extra-long indigo jeans held snugly at mid-thigh via a garter-belt that peeked beneath an A-line micro-mini in matching denim.

The angled tips of orange, 4-inch heeled sling-backs peered out from the worn bottom of the jeans. Her closed eyes were rimmed with reflective kohl edged in splatters of lapis colored paint- the only posturing at a semblance of spectacle.

Skin the color of lightly toasted bread strained against the bones of her face and the thoughts exploding behind it.

The blank-faced cinnamon-colored child sat naked staring at her maker stretching herself out up against the wall. The imprint of the dragon had been painstakingly painted across the little girl's forehead in a chalky red paste by Sector upon creation, and after many millennia was almost dry, unknown to Gera. The only other embellishments on the child's body were the glyphs of Sai-fahn branded up and down it. spelled out a story she hadn't the means to decipher. Glyphs hinting at things she somehow knew she didn't want to know. The characters were as black as the dragon on her forehead was red, and her forehead was the only space they didn't dance across due to the seal. She was nothing. Un- name-able. Unworthy of a name according to the earth Gera was formed from. Silent. Passive to the point of no return outside of annihilation. Malnourished.

No inner life had been allowed for so long that she had forgotten the ramifications of one as it began to float up to her surface. As she watched Gera go thru devic motions to pull her mind away from her rage and back into her body, the little phoenix wondered for the first time when she'd be as long and lithe as the one who claimed to be the source from which she had sprung. Silently wrapping her thoughts in imagery of fantastical horizons and beings, she wondered when the time for Gera would pass and the time for phoenix would finally arise. How the attire would suit her.

"Come here," Gera growled suddenly, motioning for Sai-fahn

with up-turned palms that had been meticulously painted with cryptograms the child couldn't read and didn't connect to the bruises branding her body.

She was too shell-shocked to comprehend that one had come from the other, and too used to pain to cringe from the physical fear that overwhelmed her at Gera acknowledging her existence. Again.

On eggshells, the diminutive child with the pitch black halo of hair approached the still stretching woman she officially knew as her creator.

"- You have nerve - are you plotting my demise so quickly, and behind such flimsy metaphors?" Gera sung softly. "Do you not believe I can hear what you think?" She smiled benevolently at the hesitant girl.

"Believe half of what you see, none that you hear-" Sai-fahn whispered, as surprised as the Gera construct was at what had fallen from her lips.

Thrown slightly off-guard, Gera waved dismissively in little phoenix's direction. Sai-fahn went careening 3o yards into the wall on the other side of the room. She landed on the floor in a heap. Blood quivered on her lip. The sheen of a shocked sweat soaked her face.

"You'd think I'd created an unbreakable fortune cookie!" Gera snapped. "This is all I get from you! - Probably all I will ever end up getting too! What a waste you are- what a waste to be assigned to watch over you-" Gera wheezed as asthmatic symptoms flared up out of nowhere, surprising Her. She slipped back into character quickly. "-At least you're not really mine -in truth, I have no bonds to your malignant ass- otherwise, I'd really be worried about my own welfare- I'd probably have to inspire you to kill yourself even earlier this time out!!" she laughed hoarsely.

Sai-fahn looked up at the Gera construct through her brows as currents of rage and pain rip-tided through her insides. The indifferent abuse had gone on for eons. The routine of the premeditated attacks had caused the Sai-fahn daemon to remain stunted in the body of a gangly eight year old. Her bruised and branded frame wore the ash of never having been shown affection. The avenues she had been domesticated to expect it from were what had made her used to a reality of terror.

She had put up with the torture for years, biding her time for a window of opportunity. She waited for the Gera construct to get lazy, sloppy like she was now. Absently, Little phoenix wiped at the sweat on her forehead- the rebellious rage stopped in its tracks by the flushed horror at the thought of smearing the red dragon yet again, She pulled her fingers back for inspection. Not a trace of the dye had come off.

Finally, the time had come.

Gera stretched her arms up to the ceiling of the cell she considered solely her domain. It was if her mind had systematically blacked out the existence of Sai-fahn as quickly as she had tossed the daemon. Suddenly the Gera construct was completely unaware of the dark eyes stalking her from its perimeter. Waiting for that precise moment when every defense had by the Gera construct was down. She had absently watched it for eons, oblivious to what she was being made privy to time and time again until now.

One by one, the Gera construct relaxed each muscle of its body. Her system cooled itself down from her outermost points towards her heart. The closer she got to that moment of ultimate relaxation, the more the noise around her threatened to push in on her from all sides. Each moment of controlled silence she got through pushed the smile more broadly across her face. Blissed.

Sai-fahn glowed.

Little Phoenix wove around the slackened mainframe of the Gera construct like a mongoose matching its movements to the breathing of a cobra. Her thoughts were direct. "Escape the Geraconstruct." Simple. Sweet. Said aloud for the first Time.

"Escape the Geraconstruct. Escape the Geraconstruct." She repeated, mantra-like. The words actually falling from the lips of the little phoenix about to plunge into the flames blocked them from registering on the radar of the Geraconstruct.

One poetic gesture.

A jack-knifed swan dive, Sai-fahn- the Little phoenix slammed her dragon emblazoned forehead into and through the still-soft spot on the crown of the one they called Gera from the blindside of the construct. The Gera construct ruptured into a deluge of coal and lapis-coated orbs, boomeranging back to and exploding on impact against the skin of the diminutive daemon Sai-fahn. More and more of the tortured flesh of the child-god burnt-off with each impact, causing her to scream as she expressed her pain openly for the first time.

When the smoke thinned, a film of glinting blue-black dust coated the child. The irises of her eyes went acid-white, blinded by the explosion. Bloodied tears rimmed her white orbs before they slid down, cutting scraggly tracks through the refuse coating her. Exhausted, the little phoenix collapsed, curled up into fetal position.

When she came out of hibernation she had already doubled in height and no longer had a name. The sound of buzzing echoed around her. The noise made her chew the inside of her jaw, and soon she was crouched on her knees, feeling along the outer edges of the cell for the source of the sound until she found a crack of white light and felt wind against the fleshy pads of her fingertips.

A stunted guffaw exploded out of her throat. The remains of construct evaporated into white.

She walked out of the memory of the cell that she had always known, fleshing out with every blue-black footprint she made in the blizzard of white noise that surrounded her, making her way to the outer limits of the Leuce-the wild forest of the inner underground that eventually sprawled out into the badlands that dropped off outside of the low end of the Empyrean. Edges of inner and outer reality peopled by unspeakable intensities. Areas of consciousness ignored in hopes they would evaporate from collective memory, never spoken of.

Now nameless, she looked down at her body, a little less detached from it with each passing of crows in the green sky above her. Absently, she rubbed roughly at the remains of skin, kneading the caked frankincense-scented soot into it. She never wanted to see any of the scars again. Not the glyphs, not the dragon- none of it. The tight coils of her hair expanded up and out. Afro-like, as if they had breathed a huge sigh of relief, that radiated an aura of harsh light.

That effulgence drew tutors to her through the badlands as if she were a premonition of what was to come. The chafing continued. The more she rubbed at her skin, the more she vocally mimicked the divergent dialects she came in contact with, the more she retained of their various Arts of War as her official mythology.

Time passed.

The soot that by this time only she saw was her armor of invisibility, earned by vanquishing a demon like the ones in the stories of her mentors. When she looked at her face in steel of hand-hammered weaponry, the features that beguiled all those who crossed her path lay hidden under layers of blackened cinders. Remnants of the cell she had destroyed only flashed occasionally in dreams that were forgotten as soon as she woke. The perception of herself as a being in her own right- apart from the atrocities of a misguided Geraconstruct- began to exist.

She was truest to herself when she was Devic. Motion was the only benevolence she knew. Movement was learned inadvertently from millennia of observing Gera, she guessed- and secretly shamed herself because of her ability. It was the furthest thing from the truth, but she had no clue. There was no one there who could comprehend enough of what she'd been through, no entity that crossed her path who could fathom her reality enough to help her separate the beauty in her from the splendor she had learned to find in the monstrous environ she had been surrounded by. It was that incomprehension and the soot that would not wash away that ran her ragged. Stripped of all else, it made the blindness real and a mercenary out of her.

She was hollow when she arrived at Messenger.

But she was welcomed. Honored as a weary warrior. Given the gifts of a full range of respect, irises slashed in a way that blocked from her ocul the soot that she saw coating her like moss. She was invincible as long as she never caught sight of herself.

Slowly she began to fathom herself as a God. She helmed the vessel of the one she had watched turn away from Gera in disgust so many lifetimes ago.

She even gave herself a lead-in name for the trip to the freedom she signed on for. Eventually she called herself Alekto, keeper of the unnamable wisdom. A luxuriously violent entity in exile, turning inside out in order to not become as wicked as what she had been led to believe she'd sprung from, the kind of spirit great cities were built for- or over.

She walked out to the edge of the territory and bent down, staring up at the tops of leafless trees that seemed to create the western perimeter, her knees and shins pressed into soft moss that went a good six feet deep. She leaned her back against the gummy bark and breathed in deeply. A raven perched on a branch high up in the tree she had chosen.

She pulled the dagger she had smashed with her bare hands and dragged it across her palm. The rivulet of blood glinted like crushed rubies and held her attention for some time.

She smoothly slid the blade into the right side of her belly and roughly dragged it back to her left side. Her head rolled down on her neck, a wet, red-winged moth made from the reflection of the scene in the shades and the sheet of blood coasting down her thighs, glinting in the light like she'd been partially coated with piles of red glitter.

chapter seventeen

In the Science and Technology Public Library on Thirty Fourth Street the drone of its media wall floated into the workstation room where Artyo sent out last respects.

Televisions blared everywhere. The media circus had already revved up and was covering the carnage in Cleveland. People gathered in front of digi-screens positioned in dirty shop windows at eye level all over the city, the gravity of it all hanging their heads low. The story was also suspended above, the eyes of the actively vindicated locked into the frenzy as if the rapture itself was raising them above the pain of living out their own personal aftermaths.

"What is going to happen to the friends of those poor people?" a random woman sighed for effect beside two followers with upturned faces before moving uncomfortably towards a cluster of more guilt-filled, shame-faced shop-window onlookers.

"Does not compute" ad campaigns sliced through the crush on the sides of buses as soon-to-be award-winning reporters gave choked up mise-en-scenes, coated in sticky blood and bark that made it seem like they were reporting from the volatile war zone they reported it all still was.

"Not this bad since the torso murders of-" a reporter bleated out. Artyo nodded in agreement as she cut her way through crowds gawking up at electronic ticker tapes, unnoticed.

"This just in- reports of a statement issued via the Internet to approximately 666 new agencies across the globe, in 13 different languages-"

Apparently, Ms. Jaymes thinks she is a *"child of god-"* worthy of redistributing God's wrath-"

The media was had such a heyday with this new topic to beat to hell that it stopped crossing anyone's mind to ask citizens to be on the lookout. Instead, Hyped up graphics announced the story on news channels that showed her personally prepared visuals spliced with interviews of old classmates.

"She always did whatever she wanted to do-"
"Never fit in-"
"Bleep" never wanted to be bothered with anybody-" "Called herself firewater or something- "

"She was always running around with all the guys - Us girls knew she was doing *something* for those boys to keep them around her all the time-"

"It doesn't makes sense- molested kids are supposed to be promiscuous- I have seen her slap the "bleep" out of someone for touching her without permission-...Oh!!!! Now I-"

Tabloid shows produced footage of second cousins, great-aunts and sundry extended family avoiding cameras and questions that main-line news-channels then shamelessly re-ran.

"Why was nothing done to protect these children?"
"Do you think Ms. Jaymes will strike your house next?" The mass funeral for the adults was televised as if it were a revolution in and of itself. Phony friends of the parents showed up for the photo-op, recording it all in person and at home in case they ended up on television.

"ABUSED CHILD/AVENGING ANGEL" splashed across international screens in bloodcurdling typeface.

"Cops aren't sure if Ms.Jaymes is still in the Cleveland area-"
"The local police have found no clues as to the-"
"Police are currently on the look-out for vigilante-"
"Last officially seen in the area ten months prior to the massacre... "

People stood frozen in front of screens suspended on the street outside of Bloomingdales. The fanatical voyeuristic activity cut deep into people who wished they could say they didn't understand what had truly gone down, coming from families racked with the same sickness that they had run to New York to get away from.

No one wanted to be conflicted as bits and pieces of the whole story fell into place. The companies that had been tied to the underground events at first thought of disavowing connections, but something made them pause. The media began to splash footage from the global grievance events across the screen in tandem with the footage Artyo had already sent out.

When company spokesmen were approached with microphones, stories started rising up out of nowhere about abuses they had lived through as kids, and how they wished they did not understand which part of this person must have snapped. When one station had the courage to run it, they all did.

Teenagers held midnight vigils for her and the progeny and burned crosses on the lawns of pedophilic parents. Then they went out and spent their parent's money on the brands that had the balls to stay connected to it all, companies that quietly made money hand over fist in the process.

The crows of NYC circled overhead as Artyo made her way uptown through Central Park, checking in on the two chosen cops that were making their rounds. She filched a bottle of communion wine from St. Patrick's on the way and drained it, the supposed blood of the highest high staining her lips.

The people living in the park made moves towards her as if they knew she was some sort of angel on sight.

They badgered her with questions they knew she had the answers to, questions that had set them out on the path of bagging it in the first place. They prayed to her as if she

were the personification of the angel of mercy right before them, blaspheming what she actually was. Their roads of the latter day warrior would be ended with one word from her. A word that, according to their rule books, she couldn't dare refuse them. But she did.

The city's future-shocked samurai began to circle her, shielding their eyes from her, begging her for peace. They scattered like leaves as the ornate communion bottle detonated at the feet of a cluster of them, embedding three with shards of glass, unable to explain why the splinters seemed as though they were pushing from within instead of out, refusing to be pulled out at area hospitals that didn't want to service them later on that night, which made the orderlies have to give them beds. She waited for the bitter taste of the spirits to take effect as she watched the haze burn off the lower end of the city.

chapter eighteen

Piccola sat staring despondently off into space. Impatient for the silence to cease, she picked up her two chrome meditation balls and threw them up against the far wall. The dented walls had been painted over with words from Ayn Rand's objectivist manifesto, scrybed in over 30 different languages and pictographs, the purity of the concepts corroded by the overwhelming amount of layers of the same information. She was so heavy-handed that she had to go and pry the metallic balls from the plaster. Their chiming thuds gave her some sort of weird comfort as they slammed into surfaces. They were the only things in her possession that she couldn't break or dent at all, no matter the abuse.

She was beautiful, not that there was anyone in the vicinity who had an appreciation of such things. The sweeping ball gown skirt, basted together by hand from remnants of antique flags from around the lower world swelled out with each step, concealing piles of the remains of guitars she smashed, postcards from around the globe, and broken albums and compact discs.

Piccola ran one French-manicured hand thru the air alongside her, the other trailing along the stitching of the Italian flag festooning the front panel of the skirt. The tightly cropped ribbed tank she wore pushed her breasts up. Pile upon pile of brightly colored African beaded necklaces wound down her de´colletage. Heavy silver bracelets snaked about her wrists and ankles. Her hair was thin and long, the color of espresso grounds, cascading down to the small of her back where it hadn't been feathered away from her face. Streaks of auburn, blue, and blond had been burned into it long ago, and they oddly complemented the tawny hue of her skin. The only makeup she appeared to wear consisted of smudges of a powdery red at her temples and in the hollows of her cheekbones.

Successfully retrieving the balls and leaving them to float on their own, Piccola waltzed herself around the pile to the rhythm of Jimi Hendrix singing about angels somewhere in the hive. As she glided through the inebriated motions, the globes followed her lead, swooshing in the air beside her, her feet occasionally tangling up in miles of discarded recording tape.

Ignoring the dance of the droning orbs done by her creator, tiny Cipher focused on the objectivist manifesto coating the wall, zoned out in the only peace she obtained in this place after an eternity of confinement. The meditation made her radiate an alien beauty, teak skin streaked with dirty sandalwood oil. Her hair grew like weed, hanging like a coarsely woven tapestry across her shoulders, the consistency and color of cotton. Her eyes seemed to slant up towards brows hell-bent on angling down at bizarre points to meet them, a beauty mark laying at the points where they would have crossed if they could have. Cipher never said a word anymore. Her lips were caked with her own blood due to truths spoken to no avail, forever stained with the things she refused to let fall from her lips for reasons not even internally discussed anymore.

Cipher was the one "made for company," the comfort child. Piccola only saw Cipher when certain tapes played in her head, when she needed a partner, a sounding board, or a punching bag. The little girl glared at the chiming chrome spheres dancing alongside Piccola, her legs tucked into lotus position under her. Piccola charted the courses of the balls. Usually, the balls would swerve to make the child recoil from their paths.

Forever this dance had been enacted. Cipher taunted by a bored, looming dancer in the Piccolaconstruct. Cipher ignoring the balls, Cipher being smacked by them. Cipher told between excited grunts from a suddenly sexually aroused Piccola that she deserved nothing more as the Piccolaconstruct beat her to a broken and bloody pulp for touching the balls, and then viciously licked the child clean. Cipher being nursed back to health by a lamenting Piccola, and then ignored until it all went down again.

A sphere careened dangerously close to the girls' head, mocking her presence. Anger welled up in her that she couldn't express since she had taken the concept of no words as the only thing she could safely own here. Another cut through the air in front of her face. Irritated for the first time in her life, the child defiantly stuck her tongue out at the mirrored surface of the ball. All movement in the room froze except for her.

She sat there in shock, eyes darting from the off-kilter Piccola balanced on one toe to the tongue reflecting back at her in the surface of the sphere. Tattooed onto the surface of her tongue were words: ***"Speak to end all evil."***

Her child-body pulled itself up and pressed itself violently into the wall. Terrified, Cipher slammed her eyes shut as the words formed on her tongue. The sound of herself saying something again exploded in her ear. "Speak to end all evil," she barked hoarsely.

The dance in the room whirled back into action as if nothing had happened. The petrified little thing rammed her body even more tightly against the wall, wishing she truly were as invisible as the Piccolaconstruct treated her most times.

The waltz ended. This was the first time an attack hadn't jumped off , and the Piccolaconstruct was a bit thrown at having a situation to raise the question of why to. She turned to find Cipher, standing stock- still against the wall.

Their eyes locked. Suspecting the child had somehow done something, her eyes narrowed. Piccola pressed play on another tape she ran from inside her head, one she knew no one- especially not the little girl, had any way to stop. Smiling a warm smile, she beckoned the child to her, settling herself down on the refuse of her inner world in a grand sweep. The child remained frozen against the wall.

Nonplussed, Piccola toyed with the full skirt made of flags and began singing aloud again. Her voice rang out into space like a nightingale's. The notes from the guitar she pulled out from under her gown and laid in her lap, playing backwards, locked onto the little girl's senses, bewitching her. Cipher shook with fear to the rhythm of the chords played. Like a pinprick that caused an inner avalanche, words slammed around inside the girl.

"We know what she wants to do, so just let her do it and be done with it!" Cipher screamed inside. As the words ran across her tiny tongue and the roof of her closed mouth, she steadied herself. The words, no matter how insane, calmed her.

Soon Piccola held her hand out to the cotton-haired child. Glee spread over her face as her mind's eye saw little Cipher doubt .. .and then shame herself, silently pulled in. Because she knew Cipher "loved" the song she was playing. But this time the little girl didn't budge.

Mystified, Piccola shifted her weight and tried the complex chords again. Cipher refused to move, strengthened inside by the sound of heavenly tongues reverberating in her inner ear. Exasperated, yet still seeing this as sport, Piccola leaned over and yanked the timid girl away from the wall by her hair.

A huge playful grin remained splayed across the cheeks of the Piccolaconstruct, flushed at the exertion. "...So you're going make me work for it this time, huh?" Piccola purred huskily. "You have the prettiest hair I've ever seen!" Piccola whispered.

All the tapes the one who eventually became the Piccolaconstruct picked up from those who malignantly pressed in on her childhood and adolescence whirled in and out of play like a remix, strategically weaving into the ultimate sell. The speed of the synch surprised her with how easily the cancerous words flew out.

"So thick! It's like heavy raw silk ... the color of clouds ... if only I had hair like that when I was your age..." Piccola said softly, mimicking the clip of toastmaster's potluck talk that had invaded Piccola repeatedly as the construct's own identity had come into being so long ago.

She ran her fingers over the head of the rigid child. Cipher's head was quiet, expectant of the end of all things as the little body braced itself for the blow.

"Aphaht tenak mehkar, surahk-Aphaht tenak mehkar, surahk-Aphaht tenak mehkar, surahk-" careened through Cipher's head. "I will Let her kill me-" Cipher suddenly thought as the cloak on the tongues lifted. She stared into the face of the woman, silent.

"You know-" Piccola purred," I worry about you... I can see already that you'll be so big! What man do you think will want something as big as- and you do realize that you move like a monster- a beast of burden... an elephant has more grace on its last ... you can never wear heels you'd be horrendous. "

Cipher just stood there and swallowed all of venom spewed.

"You probably have the nerve to think you will do any better- than I did? I'll be damned if you do- then that would mean it was never true about me either and I believed it anyway- wait- you're not better than me, dammit, you're not!!"

The Piccolaconstruct hiccupped as the tape skipped a little and sped forward, the voice momentarily sounding like it had passed through a pocket of helium. "And those huge eyes of yours? Ugh! I feel sorry for the horrible life you're going to lead. No man will ever want to be seen with you-not out in public-why would he? No way in hell-" Piccola whispered.

Cipher's eyes danced across the neck of the guitar an arm's reach away as the unrehearsed tirade picked up steam.

"You're not mine- he wanted you ... and you see what he wanted you for too, don't you- look what he let his own sister do to you-look at how it wasn't me who attacked you each time it came out as you got older- it was him- that's what he made you for- you fucking buffer-you were born with diseases from all his sluts crusted to your legs- " the Piccolaconstruct snarled.

"That's why you don't have anything-clothes- you're fucking worthless-all you do is spin in circles, It's really sad- I feel so sorry for you- NO ONE wants you! What the hell are you anyway?" the Piccolaconstruct ranted. The construct gasped as air thinned in the machinery's lungs.

The manicured hands of Piccola flew to her sternum. Her fingers fluttered nervously over the necklaces settling into her cleavage as if she was on the verge of passing out. A melodramatic crying jag threatened to erupt. Piccola's eyes narrowed as she caught the child looking at the guitar out of the corner of her eye.

"You want to ruin even more of my things?" the construct screeched. "Stay away from my things! They're Mine! Damn you! You take everything from me! I fucking hate you- you want it! Fine! Here!!" The Piccola construct picked up the guitar and slammed it into Cipher's face.

The little girl fell out into the pile of garbage. Ripped open cassette tapes dug into her flesh as she lay there praying that she'd die this time, that she'd escape the only way that seemed possible. Piccola continued to destroy the guitar over the child's frame, beating at the bones of Cipher until her arms grew weary. She tossed the decimated instrument over her shoulder and into a pile of junk she couldn't see. The little girl was bleeding to death. All over the garbage in Piccola's pristine white room in her head.

Grossed out by the splatters of blood on her skirt and tank top, Piccola wouldn't touch her. She was disgusted by the thought of getting under her fingernails the blood of the thing she had to smash in order to make it stop forcing her to say horrible things.

Piccola absently caught her breath for the addictive actions of Act Three, where all the beauty of Piccola was trampled by what had eaten her alive so long ago, the Ogre inside stretching and clawing itself out of her skin, where a half-dead cipher would go through a twisted dance of forced rebirth, still alive. Ogre Piccola would lick at the bloody girl, then shove her back under her skirt, into her womb, until she almost suffocated, her gasping at the point of death taken as a return to life in the construct.

But this time the child was happy. "I am dying," Cipher whispered to herself. She felt the blood plastering her hair to her little head in swirls as manifestoes dissolved on the insides of her eyelids.

Intermission was over.

The Ogre under the Piccolaconstruct spun around on her heels, bloated, with the bones of other devoured girls and boys in its pockets. It was woozy from the stench of blood in the air.

"What have you done to yourself- my God!" Gasping, Piccola lurched toward the girl, tawny skin now mottled, expanding with each step, the skirt of flags along the road to freedom now nothing but a skirt of black industrial strength plastic bags.

"No-!" Cipher screamed, jaws ripped open by power erupting from deep inside her. The words exploded off her tongue. "Stay the fuck away from me!" the child shrieked from the rubble.

The Ogre froze mid-lunge towards her, momentarily taken aback by the outburst. "-Shut up!" it hissed softly thru gritted, grimy,green-black teeth, looking over its shoulder as if others might somehow hear Cipher's cries after not hearing what had led up to it.

"Don't- Don't touch me! I'll fucking kill- I swear I will! Leave me the -leave me alone-Alone-" the child bawled, dragging her broken body the best she could out of the reach of the Ogre who lived under the bridge of the Piccolaconstruct.

"But you'll die! You want to die?!" The Beast yelled, indignant, as if what she offered was any kind of life.

"Don't touch me!! Stay back-" The room oscillated in and out of Cipher's focus.

"You-YOU- are... telling me what NOT to do?!" The Ogre screeched.

"Please stay away from me-" Cipher choked on blood that rose up her throat as she dragged her bruised organs across the trash-filled floor by broken limbs. She collapsed against the wall she barely made it to as she took her last breath.

Stunned, the Ogre carefully picked her way across the trashed room she could suddenly see to stand above the corpse of the little girl that got away, not knowing what to do because no tape had happened this way before. She knew that she couldn't make another by ramming a corpse back inside of herself.

It had to be alive. And she couldn't come back to life without strangling a child's life into herself if it were dead. Something in its system began to fade its garbage back into the white around it.

"Now what?" she asked the lifeless plaything at her feet. "At least now I'll never have to drag that evil thing under my skirt again." Spotting a roll of electrical tape but none of the garbage it sat upon, the Ogre sneered to itself.

Soon she had wrapped the corpse of the child up like a mummy. Smiling at its handiwork, the Ogre tossed an ornate Persian rug sloppily over the body as the shell of Piccola came to. Piccola stood up, eye to beady eye with the Ogre it had opted to feed for decades.

"Burn it!" the Ogre hissed at her. They laughed together as Piccola dug for matches. With one swipe of a match, the room burst into flames. Piccola and the Ogre screamed, writhing together in the center of the fire. Eventually, the construct was entirely gutted.

As the last embers began to diminish, a little girl that was dead crawled up atop the mountain of ashes in the room that had become her pyre, naked except for snatches of crumbling electrical tape wound around her body. She sat down cross-legged. Every twitch of muscle on her mended frame made the sticky cinders fall off her skin. She began picking at a separate piece of tape hanging halfway across her lips until she decided to leave it be. Thick hair had relaxed itself to a huge halo of white in the high heat of the blaze and swirled down her back.

A sliver of light began throbbing out from behind her, bouncing off the two metal balls at rest beside her. She assumed the half-light to be coming from them. She raised her left hand.

The orbs that had always been aimed at her face sliced up through the air and careened towards it, momentarily making her flinch before they settled softly into her palm. Cipher sat squinting at them balanced in one hand for some time, holding the piece of tape that was to become permanently adhered to her left cheek away from her mouth as she stuck out her tongue. The words were still there, even if her limbs had elongated so much that she did not recognize herself. ***Speak to end all evil.***

She suddenly became aware that the dim light in the room was seeping around the frame of a door she had never known to exist, an exit blocked by the words to freedom coined by Ayn Rand. Cipher rose and went to it, her fingers dancing around the cracks for some way to pry it open. It was a door that she walked through into white noise that washed her mind of all imagery of her death. All memories of what had happened in that place were eaten away by new sounds and sights.

And then she was standing at the path into the Leuce, naked, as so many came to it, with hair trailing down her back. She asked for something to wear only using her eyes. Her mouth was conspicuously hidden behind tape, and she had mirrored orbs levitating to her left above her shoulder blades. She christened herself Babylon. She liked it. And never could place her finger on exactly why it seemed to fit. As she walked along the top of the stone gate that marked the outer edge of Messenger, she felt the sun dappling across her cheeks through her lashes, and felt truly alive. She stopped in front of a tree and suddenly leapt at it, wrapping her thighs around the trunk and easing up it until she was perched in the highest bough. The balls floated up alongside her. Babylon bowed her body out into the wind.

She smiled and giggled like a child confidently riding a bike with no hands for the first time.

As her body careened to the bog below by choice, she felt the words on her tongue evaporate against the roof of her mouth as the Leuce was filled with her giddy laughter. The silver orbs thudded to the ground beside her body. She was the last one who needed to be released in order for Artyo to break free.

chapter nineteen

On a hill that overlooked fields of forget-me-nots poking out from under leaves months after that flower's season had passed, the women commemorating all the men in Harlem who'd lost their lives in the park since 1975 gathered to picnic in silence, in defiant communion with the blood of sons, uncles, nephews, cousins, brothers, husbands and fathers that had drenched the North area of the park. Blood that gave rise to the harshness of the red in the leaves certain times of year, the perfect shade to pass plates loaded with homemade potato salad and macaroni & cheese under. They ate in remembrance of things they never spoke about. A raised fist to God in defiance of all that seemed to run unchecked around them.

On the other side of the park, Artyo stepped back out into the city near Columbus and 107th, burying her signal in the awkward Spanglish that came alive there as another day came to an end. It was a twisted clip that she could listen to for days, straining her ears to hear what was going down in obscene tones all around her. The Spanish that his had never sounded like, that created static in her head so she could do what she had to do to be out on time.

She side-stepped piles of garbage and little kids sprawled out on the hot concrete as their friends drew outlines around their bodies in chalk, the after-effect of growing up in a world that preached they wouldn't make it past 20. It was their way of staring death in the face, or at least quietly going toe to toe with the parents who continued to ram the heresy down their throats in an attempt to keep them in line. The kids scribbled "KILL ME!" in chalk across outlines of their little bodies before running off to play funeral, their practice-as-play processions passing bullet-proofed liquor stores and hole-in- the-wall beauty salons on the way to the empty lots closest to the outskirts of the park they weren't supposed to play in.

When Artyo entered the Dominican salon of choice, the party ensuing in the place came to a halt as the 50 some odd pairs of eyes crammed into a 35-client capacity room swooped down to devour what they could before the jingling of the door chimes stopped. Everything seemed anchored to and against her presence, as if she was some sort of black hole.

Like a tape whirling back into action, the Spanglish sprinkled noise erupted as smoothly as it had ceased, in time to both the Mexican soap opera with the sound down and CD player skipping softly in the background. She sat in the first empty chair she saw, waiting for her turn to be soaped.

The shampoo girl who beckoned her silently was hardly a girl and knew who she was. Artyo was the one who tipped her for her silence when everyone else forced the poor soap- splattered woman to talk. She was a big girl, a woman everywhere except for her eyes. Tall, with hair that had been treated as her only selling point by the father who'd initially been intent on marrying her off as quickly as he'd basically sold her 8 sisters into domesticated slavery on the over- populated island. She was the darkest of the 12 children and the strongest- even including the boys. Boys the father had sent for upon finding someone to remarry him once he reached New York. Boys he valued at their worst more than he'd valued any of his daughters at their best- until he got to her.

The lies she threatened to tell on his business partners in order to gain equal passage to the states were horrendous, but they garnered his respect of her when it came to her goals. Goals that had not included being pregnant for the rest of her life, sitting around in the sweltering sun, or going stir-crazy on some arrogantly impoverished island that still couldn't collectively figure out how to keep the electricity going for more the 65% of the day, surrounded by throngs of cholitas claiming to be her friends as they sat in the air-conditioned cool of the neighborhood salon, waiting for the opportunity to stab her in the back and knock her down a peg for not regretting that she didn't come across as dainty as they all went out of their way to pretend to be, plotting to sleep with each other's husbands to pay back this and that affront as soon as given the opportunity.

"No," she thought to herself as she lathered the curiously curly hair on her sporadic client's head. "No, my goals don't include being surrounded by all this noise day in and out. But at least I've gotten to New York. And I could get into school if i studied hard enough. And move to some place where there wouldn't be another Dominican around for days. *like West Jersey*," she mused to herself.

Artyo let out a giggle, causing the big, silent woman to jump in horror as if her thoughts had been overheard. She eyed Artyo suspiciously before she realized that wherever the woman was, it certainly was nowhere near where she was getting her hair done.

As the shampoo girl pointed her back over to the styling stations, she noticed how hot her hands always were upon scrubbing that one's hair even though she'd been washed in cool water. And as usual, the thought was gone as quickly as a new head appeared at the chair in front of the sink.

Folding her frame up to fit long legs under the counters lining

Mirror Image salon, Artyo waited the way she always did, eyes closed to the silent bickering between the youngest stylists over who would be forced to do her hair.

They murmured about how the owner of the salon treated her and only her like she was an honored guest.

But today the oddly honored guest was impatient.

She spun around on the cluster of young girls, teeth bared, sizing them up as if she was about to eat them alive. The one she pointed to was like a dead man walking over to her, eyes serene, not knowing what to expect as she approached the back of her head.

Her fingers trembled before touching the hair, the pained look on her face contorting to confusion as she ran both hands through it, breaking out into a grin as it registered that she'd never felt anything like it. The hair seemed to move with a life force of its own. Chunks of hair had been hacked at arbitrarily, some sections resting above an ear, some dropping in coils past her shoulders. As Artyo settled into the chair, the stylist suddenly felt very important. She made a pact to do as the hair told her to, strangely stopping short of crossing her latent Catholic heart as she usually did when making promises as such. She shook it off and got to work.

The drone of the dryers mixing with the angular Spanish bounced off the mirrors as the stylist worked on her. Artyo zoned out, focused on the outdated hairstyle posters on the walls and the craggily lilt of the old woman singing along with Marc Anthony a few chairs over from her. She floated in the static in her head due to the roar of the hair-drying unit pulled down over it.

Those tracking her through sector struggled to make a lock on her whereabouts, terrified that she was consciously blocking out her signal, and that she might be somewhere in Tokyo, near him, able to intercept. If the council had been able to come together across spiritual-political-spatial language lines drawn in the sand, they would not be having this problem.

It was bad enough he had taken to surrounding himself with gaijin hustlers of every nationality possible, making it that much harder for them to figure out he had indeed been back in Japan. But Thyaz had made it worse by picking up a kind of Japanese that had been almost indecipherable to them, giving the effect of a perverted, confused and stupid middle- aged salariman. But the fact that even in Thyaz's impending death she refused to burn across the radar- that she could consciously figure out a way to block- was obscene.

"What the hell is that?!" the tracker screamed over the din crackling through their homing device, threatening to burn it out. His partner screamed as blood began spilling from his ear, a signal they'd be punished with absolution for losing after taking so long to find.

Artyo's eyes flickered in the mirror. Absently, her left hand scratched at the slowly healing gash across her right jugular.

"What the-" stammered the stylist, catching sight of the slash mark on her wrist and snatching the hand from her throat to make sure she wasn't imagining what she was just now seeing. Artyo's eyes locked with the hail-marrying young girl in the mirror.

"Just- do- the hair-!" she growled at the girl loud enough for only her to hear. The stylist stood frozen, wanting to do nothing else but to go away from this person who looked like she should be dead the closer you peered into those eyes that she suddenly couldn't tear away from. She just wanted to go home. On the verge of sobbing, the stylist put the finishing touches on the head in front of her.

Backing away from her slowly she slammed into Viernesa, the

owner of the salon.

Artyo sat slouched in the spinning chair, sinewy arms and legs shooting out from its confines and taking up more space than seemed to make sense.

The only ones that didn't seem to mind were the chalk dust covered kids who dashed in and around her trying to keep up with that afternoon's running mates. As she stood up to pay, a straggling kid tore past her, making her lift up her leg in order for him to escape any type of collision.

The little boy stopped, turned and looked up at her, curious that the ghost had felt the need to move out of his way. She looked just as precociously at him for trying to run through her. The boy paused as if listening to someone no one but him

and Artyo could see as it bent down to his level, explaining her to him. His mouth dropped open softly and the boy nodded at her in understanding before turning on his heels and dashing back out of the door.

Artyo made her way over to Viernesa and the still shaken stylist, who had been imploring the owner not to make her take the blackened money of whatever had sat down in her Seat.

"How much?" Artyo said stiffly.
"On the house, mahmi," the owner whispered, looking into Artyo's hollowed out eyes. Viernesa touched the hair that was so much like her own hair that she'd have made the girl she had known long before seeing her face on the news last night her child if she could have, if it would have made any difference.

"Thank you," Artyo grumbled, bowing her head softly in respect to the older one that had made it through. She received a kiss on the forehead from the beautiful crone in return then walked over to the shampoo girl and shoved a wad of money that she wouldn't need any more into the woman's apron pocket. "To see past Jersey," She whispered, on the other side of the salon before the surprised woman could say a word.

The sun was orange again as it began to slowly fall from the sky. Slashes of warm light soothed the skin on Artyo's cheek as she pulled the D/A/P out and broke the wax, placing the coin-printed bindi-like dots over her temples to hold whatever it turned out to be in place until she got where she needed to be.

Tossing the tiny chunks of wax away, she was out the door. The bells above the door jingled as the salon grew silent once again at her departure. Before any questions came up, Viernesa whipped everyone back up into light celebration as if nothing of import had passed. She never thought about the fallen angel again.

chapter twenty

The surge of media attention on the massacre continued with even less concern about tracking down the still at large killer who was immediately dwarfed by the response of the masses.

The 6th floor sex crimes unit of Cleveland's downtown precinct was like a bunker. Public relations specialists were brought in to maneuver through the landmines that exploded with every step the detectives took to cover tracks on this case and others like it they had never given much thought to in the past. The callous dealings that were the norm with people "trying to help" those who already were seen as victims finally began to see the light of day. Reporters camped out at all building exits and on the off-ramps at car-parks the officers stored their civilian vehicles in, flinging themselves on hoods in hopes of pushing cops to start giving out citations.

Surprising factions joined the mourning as it was slowly turning into an uproar. The spin-doctors had expected drama and reactive outrage from the younger generation and had focused all their energy in keeping them in check.

Kids watched as their unoffending parents morphed into paranoid fundamentalists at the possibility that something they had done in moments of anger long ago would come back through the hands of children who had no complaints against them, thanks to the visual inoculation on the nightly news that focused on the small segment of violence actually coming through the under eighteen segment of society versus the colossal explosion of activity in the parental and professional sectors, a calculated skewering of the actual reality akin to the percentage of crimes actually committed by young black males versus the number of times such crimes made the news.

The stories of the discarded bodies of poisoned children and kids who had been suffocated in their sleep were overlooked. Every crime purportedly perpetrated by a minority of any category was in rotation on the news and across ticker-tapes an average of 666 times more often than the rising tide of rage erupting from middle-class males and females across the globe, quietly justifying lobbying efforts stateside to swoop down with emergency legislation that could effectively take away the rights of women and minorities for the sake of restoring societal order.

Old boys clubs were packed with men smoking cigars as the countdown to the House of Representatives and Senate races kicked off, hoping their constituents would get swept up into the panic the media was orchestrating, knowing the option of martial law would work in their favor.

The premeditated media focus left them completely unprepared for the explosive pockets of uprisings that came from the religious sector. Clusters of the adults who had spoken out against the church paying off their parents regarding the sexual abuse by clergy went berserk, burning down the homes and destroying the other emblems of the "better life" their parents had bought with the hush money given to them for turning a blind eye to the attacks against their own kids.

Churches of every denomination were mobbed, crowded to the rafters full of fear-soaked people, or firebombed in the night, depending on the state of things in the communities they had laid foundations within.

Statues of saints were toppled and smashed. Clergymen who had been relocated instead of dismissed were tracked down and murdered in cold blood. Religious fanatics who were normally so quick to scream about the beginning of the Apocalypse went into virtual comas as the possibility of this being the big one slammed into them like a ton of bricks, angry at their personal Gods suddenly offering no comfort, questioning them instead on painful events in their pasts that had led them to hide away so deeply in whichever dogmas or rituals they had chosen as their havens. A deluge of professionals mobilized to speak out on the issue after years of guilt, depression, self-medication and repressed rage. Baby boomers began dropping like flies as a twisted new kind of passion crime erupted over the public radar.

"Average Joe" professionals began snapping in major markets, taking impromptu trips back to hometowns they had long ago left behind to confront the senior citizens that had once been the banes of their existences. Men who had been abused as children and had in turn grown up to beat their wives and lovers begged for forgiveness as the children they had spawned took their lives gangland-style on behalf of past bruises, broken bones and beat down mothers.

Underground, discotheques and nightclubs became the equivalent of fallout shelters as the urgent need for escape grew to horrendous proportions. Those living on the fringe thanked god for already having relieved them of the need to go back and face the parents who had forsaken them, for giving them peace and ecstasy and tiny little k-holes to crawl into to keep them motivated to live another day.

Black-market prices for all types of self-medicated relief skyrocketed as club-door policies became stricter and stricter. Clubland had enough strains of insanity woven into it by its very nature to not succumb to the pressure of above.

Those fighting for some semblance of control in the world of day-trippers kept trying to pin the tail on the purported hedonism of the underground. But this time, they weren't putting this shit off on those hiding out below because there was no way in hell any more of them were getting in to plant anything.

The underground became impenetrable. The powers that be officially became as impotent above as they had always been below. They came up empty-handed as they looked for causes and reasons of marketable societal Putrefaction in the alleyways and parking lots of nightlife districts across the country- because beasts were blooming exactly where they had been sown- in homes across the good ole United States of America.

The real action was already burning like a sack of shit on the precious front porches of the homes people were fearfully sneaking out the back doors of. The media gorged itself in the feeding frenzy of violence and pre-meditated gore as adult children of abusers became God's judgment against parents who believed there was no retribution allowed for atrocities enacted under the guise of ignorance, and broadcast it to every corner of the world in vivid detail.

chapter twenty one

Soigne´ dragged a paint smeared hand across the stubble on his bald-by-choice head, depositing a streak of blue beside the flecks of red and green from earlier layers of his latest work that rested against the easel.

His lanky frame hung from an impressive spread of shoulders, defiantly, as if he refused the assignment of perfection in the Empyrean by keeping a gauntness about him. He stood in badly bruised combat boots found at the closest thing the plane had to a dump, the only area in the realm he saw as infused with the remnants of life and lives lived, however paltry. The dingy long john bottoms that hung loosely from his hips had received the brunt of many a paint- streaked palm and overloaded brush to make them so. The tiny coils at the center of his birch-colored chest were the only unadjusted hairs on him. Besides his expertly arched brows, he amped up his eyes with the application of falsies at the end of each forced recalibration no matter how thickly the hairs lining his lids had become in protest to him adding to their take on how beautiful he was meant to be.

His eyes glinted with the fire of a creative geist that had been initially deemed as removable in the Empyrean realms but had kept cropping up like a more powerful second bald head for the Angel with no other Eloh to speak of other than his Art, especially in the absence of other tendencies that had also been deigned removable. Soigne´ seemed irrevocably wired not to experience the variant of shame those in power had been so used to relying upon once his sort actually got to "the highest high possible."

The workshop was cramped, coated with dust, acrylic and tempura. Old gray easels he had rescued from the dump filled in the shadows piled up against the walls.

The still brilliant colors that danced across their discarded frames were the closest he saw to sanity in a so-called heaven, the texture of the splintering and peeling pigments the only things he actually still felt. Shafts of red daylight were diffused into the nearest he could get to natural light by layers of translucent scrims across windows. Splatters of paint that mutated into peculiar vistas and bodhi-filled landscapes played out opposing dramas against the floorboards and walls.

The latest in a series of half-baked cloaked propaganda posters the Tryage had "commissioned" from him was his showing of camaraderie within the Empyrean sat piled awkwardly in the middle of the floor. He had to trample them repeatedly to gain freedom of movement within his own personal womb, and did so to ensure he never forgot the truth of where he was, no matter what they tried to sell otherwise.

The unfinished image of IIrys as she looked out at him over her shoulder loomed out from the canvas in front of him. Her eyes were wild with the reality of a foreseeable escape that he hadn't understood the import of when she asked him to capture what she had felt when she was in the middle of it, her lips ripped open with the obscene knowledge of a loophole only his defiant muse would be insanely courageous enough to take so early in the game.

He saw the imprint of his palm square in the center of her unfinished back in the built-up white of the painting. Saw how his private expression here had been instrumental in leading her to her own way out. She had made Soigne´ promise he'd finish it no matter what happened and deliver it to her Elohim Anadyr, but he hadn't worked on it since he heard the panicked whisper of how the Anadyr he had not yet met up with had been restrained and recalibrated by the Cossacks the Tryage sent after they caught him trying to burn all of his perfect things that no longer had meaning.

In that moment Soigne´ had put on his own mantle of heavenly shame and vowed to himself to never factor into that entities' pain ever again, and stopped working on the only portrait she had asked of him. He hadn't requested the assistance of nor felt the need for a replacement muse since. And the few landscapes he painted in the dearth that followed her absence were so sub-par that he was insulted with the art of his own hand. He had felt as if finally this place had hollowed out the one thing that had kept him alive in this vacuum.

Until the last eon was over.

He suddenly found himself pulled into the dusty workspace he had no Eloh to share with, the desire to paint so intense in his fingertips that the line-less palms of his hands had felt coated with creative fire. His energy spewed out of his refracted tear ducts in the place of tears with every gash across the canvas. The echo of moist paint as it dropped through the air and splattered on the floor was joyous revelry.

He made a heavenly mess and loved every moment of it. Thoughts of how life alone after death could occasionally be beautiful danced through his head as they usually did when he was somewhere within the orbit of pseudo-joie d'apres- vivre. What had made him pause was the sudden introduction of a wayward thought -the possibility of life after the after-life. Soigne´ cocked his head to the side and his jaw slid open in shock.

"*ooh-no Ms.thing dint-*" formulated just enough on the inner lid of his eyes to pre-empt him speaking the syllables aloud. He always knew he was being watched.

The heavenly cascade of bells exploded behind him.

Begrudgingly, he tucked away his realization that yes MS. thing's crazy ass indeed had, and went to answer the call from above. He dragged both hands across the indentation at the back of his skull to calm himself enough to press into the exoID unit on the door without causing any unnecessary alarms about the source of any perceived excitement. The door swung open and the silence that came with it was as chaotic, as forced as the cacophony that proceeded it. He gritted his teeth, bent over and retrieved the "reminder" package.

Soigne´ looked down at the thick lapis lazuli pigment on the fingertips that held the gilded translucent envelope that had just been delivered to him. It registered that yet another assignment was held in his hands, another moronic duty the powers that be wished to use to silently ensure fewer Angels alongside him would follow his private path to "glory," for fear of being put to work. The reminder of the Strands- the awarding the latest Comptroller assignments, got tossed onto the floor.

He'd get ready when he was ready to go.

He tuned his inner ear for any pirated updates and got back to finishing the portrait. It suddenly seemed he was going to keep his deferred promise to IIrys after all.

Soigne´ slammed out of the house and pushed deeper into the crowd that fell away. Petals of garishly bright flowers got caught up in wind machines positioned in the polished sewer grates that skipped along the surface of the streets. Each time a voice belled in his ear, Soigne´ gritted his teeth down even harder and tried not to think legible thoughts that would easily be attributed to him in the aftermath of what he was about to do. An aggravated indignant sheen began to pimple his bare forehead. Soigne´ traveled in the crush close to the empty canal that cut diagonally across the realm towards its processional edge. The entire Empyrean was on alert for incoming, potential arrivals, crossovers.

chapter twenty two

Anadyr was still pissed at how anticipation of getting out of the house had spurred him into gear and had even gotten him there on time for the appointed second-guesting. And he was uneasy about how much time he had spent trying to make himself look like the worst rep of a hellishly designed 'Heaven' he could possibly be. To him, the crowds were the equivalent of an emulsion of spirit whisked together to give the appearance of the most heavenly garnish or flavor to the giant soundstages they melodramatically acted out their respective sacred plays on with one another. But when it came down to it, they were only quietly contained beads of lost energy and light that were unable to register let alone truly blend with each other. The Empyrean was coated in the spiritual equivalent of gourmet mayonnaise.

He hated the press of crowds; even crowds of beings programmed never to touch another being, and had arrived on the causeway with his reflective aviators and a snarl in place, ready to overwhelm the randomly assigned newbie with his thinly veiled diffidence. Anadyr pulled a bottle of enzyme water out of his back thigh pouch and took a huge swig of it without missing a beat.

"This is still the smoothest route to where we need to be-" he said to himself between gulps. He placed the bottle back without second thought as he angled this way and that to move through the entities that surrounded him. The crowds congealed towards the processional gardens at the edge of the realm. The somehow tranquil gash of violently red atmosphere hung above their heads. The pieces and parts of minced flower heads swam lazily in air currents a few notches above them alongside gigantic, sleepy-eyed crows that took in the whole crush as if smirking.

chapter twenty three

Eyeing the sun's position in the sky, Artyo made her way back to the top of the park along Cathedral Parkway, St. John's looking down on her for the last time.

As if directed by the child who'd been told by his Angel, the children had littered the sidewalks of the trail she took with the little outlines of their dead and dying bodies, altering the outlines with the addition of wings rendered as if pushed down through snow, scribbling smiley faces and "GOODBYE!!" across them.

Artyo slashed through the air. The city was a broken-down machine. Anger exploded up so harshly that it made her cough up a mixture of blood and communion wine, the last of her hatred for the plane splattering itself across her lips and distorting the music in her head.

She re-focused on the sound of Bronx-Style Bob's Retribution blaring in her ears. In her mind's eye, she could see the two cops making their way towards their altar to be, timing it out against the final guitar riff of the song before she'd be gone. She made her way into the trees.

A bag lady new to the park but not the life called out to her from within the ocean of the junk she called her things. She was on a bench a few yards off to the right, pleading with her for some change to buy some salve for her swollen feet without even looking up, only responding to the sound of feet crumpling through the leaves nearby. It had been the word salve that had stopped Artyo. Made her look back. As she paused, Thyaz's voice split through her head like a bolt of lightning, whipping her body around and throwing her off balance.

"-I-I-KNOW YOU CAN BEAR-...CAN HEAR-NE-" Thyaz's voice exploded behind her left eye, sending her reeling as if she had just been punched in the midst of a migraine.

Everything inside her went silent. The bag lady, registering that the motion around her had stopped, looked up expectantly, seeing what she had called out to for the first time.

"What-do-you-NEED?!" Artyo screamed at her.

"Something-mmma-my feet-" the old woman went on stupidly, pointing down to the engorged blistered things she'd grown accustomed to. "I-can't- get my shoes on no more-" she whimpered like a child.

Artyo bent down without saying a word, closing her eyes to the pain still throbbing in her head as she unlaced her boots and tossed them at the foot of the mountain of other things the woman had acquired over the years.

"Hock them and HEAVEN or HELL won't hide you- " Artyo snarled softly as the woman dove for the square-toed lace up boots with the three inch heel that would be two sizes too big, exactly the two sizes she currently needed.

She looked up at Artyo, nodding her head in sheepish disbelief as Artyo turned on her bare heels and headed into the woods, stepping on green glass that cut the bottom of her numb feet as she did. The sun was setting but the sky refused to get dark. Bronx-Style Bob sang out when the two cops were within sight, maybe 40 yards away from her.

"Nothing I know from the sea to the sand-," The pop of static in her head once again erupted, 100 times harder, making Artyo scream out in pain as she crashed to her knees.

"I CANT TAKE THIS ANYMORE-" Thyaz screamed, the world before her going white before dissolving into a play by play of him picking a fight with a pack of yakuza thugs who were known and avoided even by the local Tokyo police, at 830 in the morning in the basement of a hostess bar. It was violence he and his Ka had consciously hunted for, both all the more alive the closer he got to death.

"I Don't-KNOW-THIS HAPPENED- I'M SORRY-"Thyaz screamed inside his own head to her as drops of blood seemed to come through her cheeks exactly where she could see they had smashed his face in. "I KNOW YOU - FORGIVE ME." Then there was nothing but the sound of an off-line TV station signal erupting in her head.

"Ma'am, are you okay?" The first cop shouted over the din upon reaching her, taking care not to touch the partially exposed dark skin of her chest as he shoved her backward to get a better view of her face, his hand already on the trigger, opportunistic about the possibility of firing into something black again.

Her head snapped up, body following as she locked eyes with and landed a fierce upper-cut on the taken aback cop, knocking him to the ground. She locked eyes with his stunned partner thirty paces away. Both officers froze in response to the crack of bullets that woke them up to the fact that she had taken the downed cops gun.

"Miss! Please!" the downed cop screamed as she raised the gun up and fired a spray of bullets at the still armed man, hitting him in the hand and shoulder and throwing him backward. "Miss! PLEASE! WHATEVER IT IS- WE CAN DO SOME-"

"What the hell! What the hell!" The bleeding man screamed as she lowered her aim to the cowardly cop that was still holding all of his blood inside him, wishing he could say the same for the urine running down his pants.

"WHAT THE HELL! WHAT THE HELL!!" screamed the bleeding cop, praying that he'd go into shock so the pain would go away, thoughts of those fourteen innocent black boys he'd gotten away with killing this fiscal year swirling around him as if they were actually there, waiting for him to die so they could drag him down to hell where all the others he'd gone free for killing in the name of the law would be waiting for him.

"Please! PLEASE!! WHATEVER YOU'RE THINKING OF DOING! DON'T MAKE THIS ANY WORSE-"

"Bam." she scoffed as a bullet exploded in the right ankle of the cop with no reachable weapon. He screamed out in pain. She laughed. The homeless men who'd spent years being pistol-whipped with no relent stood atop the hill in the distance, ears piqued to the blasts, blandly wondering who else would be found dead the next day, full of 15th and 12th precinct bullets.

At the annual picnic of the mothers of the neighborhood's slaughtered men, little children who would be the first to grow up and know life without the harassment of these particular two men in blue began to whirl around like spinning tops between the blankets laid out on the ground, speaking in tongues as the matriarchs fanned themselves, sweating profusely like they had suddenly been transported to some tinderbox of a Baptist church just ignited by the Holy Ghost.

"Tell your partner to go for his gun." She whispered softly to the unarmed cop.

"WHA-T?" he whimpered hoarsely.
"Tell you partner to go for his gun! " She snapped evenly.

"YOU SHOT HIM, YOU STUPID BITCH-!!" He screamed, bitch getting caught in his throat as a smirk spread across her face. "I'm so-I'm so- sorry-" he stuttered.

"Bam." The left knee of the second cop exploded under a hail of bullets.

His vision went all blurry as he rolled to his side, vomiting his lunch onto the already blood soaked leaves. Crows cracked up overhead.

The first downed cop went delirious, screaming at ghosts of all the young men he had killed over the years that were not there, souls he was sure were trying to drag him to face Satan.

The second cop flailed around like a fish freshly out of water, choking on his own puke. She looked at two of them twitching on the ground they'd hallowed via the killing of so many innocents over the past 25 years, and the crippling of so many others via guns they sold to dealers who recruited in the area rank and file.

The two cops had been the beginning of a plague that became the norm for the city, they had known it, and had planned to retire from the force early enough to enjoy the spoils from it.

The first police officer had a heart attack in the fallen leaves from fear of facing his version of God. He had received flesh wounds in the shoulder and hand by his partner's gun and would have survived with minute scarring.

The second cop snorted up his own vomit in surprise as Artyo cursed in disgust over them and stuck the barrel of his gun in her mouth, rammed it down her throat and pulled the trigger, exploding into a burst of light.

He died from drowning, hyperventilating as he watched Artyo evaporate in a glimmering arc of blood and light right in front of his eyes.

The end.

ABOUT THE AUTHOR

Author and multimedia artist Angel Brynner has marched to the beat of her
own drum across the arts for over two decades. After formal training with
the vanguard of the menswear industry she helmed her own line of men's
clothing and produced events for the collection in the club scenes of
New York and Tokyo.

She became quietly known for the futuristic cautionary tales back-dropping
her collections, taking over clubs and the guerilla-marketing style she used
to slam her vision into the hearts of her fans. While being sponsored by
Multinational companies desiring audience with her underground tribe, she
returned from Japan to her hometown to press charges against a pedophile
before the statute of limitations ran out.

Cast as a vigilante by a corrupt sex crimes unit for trying to protect another
child from the same attacker, during the media onslaught against
the first brave adults to come forward and press charges against
the Catholic priests that had abused them as children she was hit with a
vision of all those already lost in a sick war on kids no one talked about.

She committed herself & her art to doing something about it.

The grievechronic universe was forged in the fires of imagining the
Armageddon that would erupt through a generation of kids who
had finally had enough abuse at the hands of adults and
banded together under their grievances.
The epic spiritual, metaphysical, and historical implications
of such an event played out on every level- from the hellish norms
that caused it to what would be called heaven by such a broken world-
made her head spin.

Published by Kokopellima Press, each free-standing installment of grievechronic
Is a take-no- prisoners tale.

Alongside AOLAB[the active-art series featuring the multimedia work
that fed Eutaxis, Ecclesia, Exodus, Erebus, Exist and the kinetic collection
of novels that follow them], Angel Brynner's books are the culmination of
an artistic journey many years in the making,
all leading to a mysterious future project entitled **Transcendence.**

The first THREE books of the /grievechronic\ series

EUTAXIS ECCLESIA EXODUS

Are now exclusively Available in audiobook form

@ elevenreader.io

Books Series

Eutaxis. /Grievechronic\ book one.

Angel Brynner

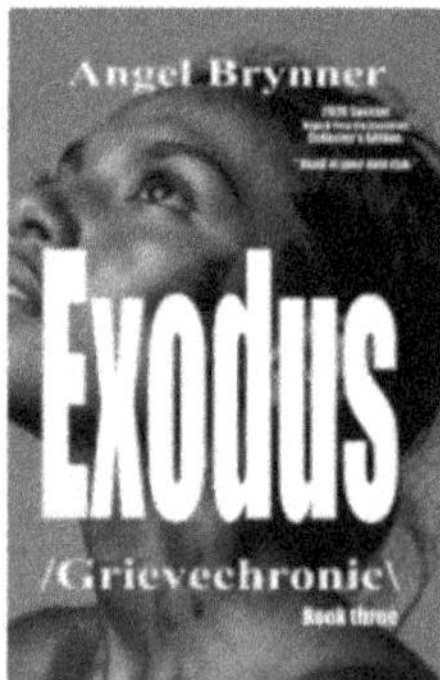

EXODUS. /grievechronic\ book three.

Angel BRYNNER

ECCLESIA. /grievechronic\ book two.

Angel BRYNNER

Books   Series

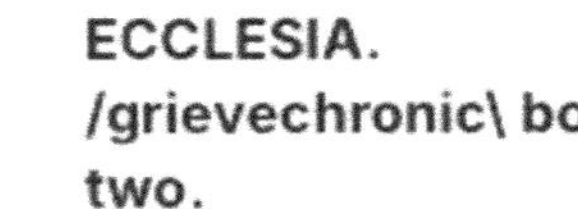

Eutaxis. /Grievechronic\ book one.

Angel Brynner

EXODUS. /grievechronic\ book three.

Angel BRYNNER

ECCLESIA. /grievechronic\ book two.

Angel BRYNNER

Angel Brynner

fire
starter
covid compendium

fire
walker
c o v i d compendium
by Angel
Brynner

...Coming soon~

THE NINTH (& LATEST) ENTRY TO THE /
GRIEVECHRONIC\ UNIVERSE

False utopias look like heaven when they exist
inside of you, but the spell breaks when you
fall. Halcyon days harbor great space for
healing if they can stand being held up to the
light. The memories we run and hide in may
overlap or coincide, but underneath each
pleasing space is all that we have yet to face.
Hiding bodies to embrace the good is par for
the course. But those bones must live again in
order to truly break free. The good goes down
in spite of what you have to ignore to be
grateful for it, but ignoring shit doesn't make
anything really go away….and going away
only goes so far.

"It looks like Heaven." That may be true. But
don't forget what you've gone through

Elysum

before or after the fall may never have been Paradise at all.

ISBN 978-1-950077-83-0

52000

9 781950 077830

Angel Brynner
ELYSUM
/grievechronic\
Now available in paperback
Everywhere.

9 781950 077632